MW00413870

CONTENTS

Case of the
Unlucky Emperor

By

J.M. Poole

Sign up for Jeffrey's newsletter to get
all the latest corgi news—
AuthorJMPoole.com

BOOKS BY
JEFFREY M. POOLE

Cozy Mystery
CORGI CASE FILES
Case of the One-Eyed Tiger
Case of the Fleet-Footed Mummy
Case of the Holiday Hijinks
Case of the Pilfered Pooches
Case of the Muffin Murders
Case of the Chatty Roadrunner
Case of the Highland House Haunting
Case of the Ostentatious Otters
Case of the Dysfunctional Daredevils
Case of the Abandoned Bones
Case of the Great Cranberry Caper
Case of the Shady Shamrock
Case of the Ragin' Cajun
Case of the Missing Marine
Case of the Stuttering Parrot
Case of the Rusty Sword
Case of the Unlucky Emperor

Epic Fantasy
BAKKIAN
CHRONICLES
The Prophecy
Insurrection
Amulet of Aria

(coming soon from Secret Staircase Books)

(coming soon from Secret Staircase Books)

ACKNOWLEDGMENTS

I drew from a lot of experience for this book, both from my Alaskan cruise earlier this year which, conveniently enough, stopped in Sitka, to my years of being a zoo keeper. So, first off, a major thank you goes out to Point Defiance Zoo & Aquarium, in Tacoma, WA. It still remains as one of my favorite places to work. Granted, it's been a number of years, but who's counting? As always, I also need to thank my wife, Giliane, for her help in prodding my memory and fleshing out several characters. I don't know what I'd do without her.

I also need to thank the members of my Posse, for going through the story and pointing out some glaring mistakes. Jason, Caryl, Carol, Elizabeth, Michelle, you guys rock! Also, thanks go out to my beta readers at Secret Staircase Books: Sandra, Susan, Marcia, Paula, and Isobel.

And you, the reader. You have my thanks. Thanks for the kind words, encouraging requests to keep the series going, and the stories (and pics!) you send me of your own fur babies. I can safely say that Zack, Jillian, and the dogs will have many more adventures. You never know what can happen in a small town!

Hope you enjoy the story! Happy reading!

DEDICATION

For Giliane -

No further words are necessary.

CORGI CASE FILES

CASE OF THE

UNLUCKY EMPEROR

BOOK 17

J.M. POOLE

Secret Staircase Books

Case of the Unlucky Emperor
Published by Secret Staircase Books, an imprint of
Columbine Publishing Group, LLC
PO Box 416, Angel Fire, NM 87710

Copyright © 2023 Jeffrey M. Poole
All rights reserved. No part of this book may be reproduced or
transmitted in any form or by any means, electronic or mechanical,
including photocopying, recording, or by an information storage and
retrieval system without permission in writing from the publisher.

This book is a work of fiction. Names, characters, places and incidents
are either the product of the author's imagination or are used fictitiously.
Any resemblance to actual events or locales or persons, living or
dead, is entirely coincidental. Although the author and publisher
have made every effort to ensure the accuracy and completeness of
information contained in this book we assume no responsibility for
errors, inaccuracies, omissions, or any inconsistency herein. Any
slights of people, places or organizations are unintentional.

Book layout and design by Secret Staircase Books
Penguin graphics in chapters by Punnawich Limparungpatanakij

First trade paperback edition: January, 2023
First e-book edition: January, 2023

* * *

Publisher's Cataloging-in-Publication Data

Poole, J.M.
Case of the Unlucky Emperor / by J.M. Poole.
p. cm.
ISBN 978-1649141200 (paperback)
ISBN 978-1649141217 (e-book)

1. Zachary Anderson (Fictitious character)—Fiction. 2.
Amateur sleuth—Fiction. 3. Sitka, Alaska—Fiction. 4. Pet
detectives—Fiction. 5. Penguin breeding—Fiction. I. Title

Corgi Case Files Mystery Series : Book 17.
Poole, J.M., Corgi Case Files mysteries.

BISAC : FICTION / Mystery & Detective.

813/.54

ONE

Autumn had to be, without a doubt, my absolute favorite time of the year. The temperatures were brisk in the morning. The leaves on all the surrounding trees were pulling out all stops with their bright reds, oranges, and even yellows. A simple walk outside was the perfect way to enjoy the crisp fall air and the vibrant colors Mother Nature was more than willing to provide. Days were getting shorter, and you could almost taste the snow in the air.

Granted, in our neck of the woods in southwestern Oregon, we didn't get that much of the white stuff. Maybe a few inches a year. However, it typically didn't stay cold enough here for it to last more than a few days.

Before I go any further, I guess I should

introduce myself. My name is Zachary Anderson, but just about everyone calls me Zack. I live in the small town of Pomme Valley, and if you don't know where that is, I'll tell you how to find us on a map. Find Medford, which is the largest southern city, about forty miles north of the California border, and then look slightly southwest. See it now? You might have to either whip out a magnifying glass, or if you're the newer generation, zoom in a bit. See? I told you it was small. Pomme Valley, or PV to the locals, has a population that barely breaks three thousand. Normally, I'd balk at living in such a small town, but thanks to Medford's proximity, everything we could possibly need is less than ten minutes away: mall, restaurants, hotels, and even a (tiny) international airport.

I've been living in this town since I learned I had inherited a private winery—and all the necessary land—from my late wife's family. Oh, don't get me wrong. The previous owner's family did everything they could to make my life miserable, figuring I had no right to lay claim on anything of theirs. Well, the matriarch of the family, one Bonnie Davies, had given *explicit* instructions for her entire estate to be left to me and my wife. Thanks to Samantha's unfortunate death, resulting from a horrible car crash, that left only me.

Long story short, I ended up moving from my home in the hot Arizona desert and relocating to the much cooler Pacific Northwest. I was originally unsure how I was going to like it, and let me tell you, the first week had me second-guessing my recent life choices. After all, getting falsely accused of murder does have a tendency to sour one's perception on your new home. Within twenty-four hours of stepping foot in PV, I was arrested for murder and thrown in jail. Thankfully, just before that happened, an old school friend of mine, who also happened to be living in PV, talked me into adopting a dog. Thanks to my furry companion, I avoided getting blamed for the murder.

Sherlock's unique ability managed to keep me out of ... sorry, I'm getting ahead of myself. My two dogs require an explanation, or else you're going to think I'm off my rocker. And yes, there are two, so let me explain.

As I mentioned, I have two dogs, who are named Sherlock and Watson. Both are corgis. Those unfamiliar with the breed will be wondering what they are. Those who do recognize the breed will be asking if they're Pembroke or Cardigan. They're Pembrokes, the ones which typically don't have a tail. Remember the Queen of England and her favorite dogs? Those are the corgis I'm talking about.

I adopted Sherlock first, just because I'm a sucker and apparently can't say no to my friend, Harrison Watt. He's the town veterinarian and is responsible for running PV's canine rescue center, too. Anyway, he talked me into taking on the tri-colored furball that apparently had a problem with authority. The two of us took to each other straight away, and much to my amazement, Sherlock demonstrated to me he had an innate talent: sniffing out clues that are somehow related to whatever case I'm working.

Sherlock kept my tail out of jail, found the actual murderer, and even located a priceless sculpture that had been stolen. In case you're wondering why he isn't working for the police department, well, he is. All three of us. Watson, my little girl, isn't quite as talented as Sherlock in the *sniffing for clues* department, but she can still hold her own. She's a sweet, cuddly girl who loves to snuggle up next to her daddy for some belly rubs.

That's usually when she lets one rip. Watson eats too fast, which causes a build-up of air in her tummy and, well, the air has to go *somewhere*. I'm working with her on trying to get her to slow down her eating. No one likes to have their eyeballs melt in their sockets from the smell of rotten broccoli.

The final thing I should mention about myself, aside from being a winery owner and a police consultant, is that my main profession is that of a writer. A romance writer, if you can believe that. But, don't go looking for my name on any of the dozens of books I've published. I always use aliases for every book I write. For my romance novels, I go by Chastity Wadsworth. Yep, it's a woman's name. Mock all you want, but my royalty checks alone each month afford me quite a lavish lifestyle.

Speaking of lifestyles, it was also the main reason I found myself in the situation I was currently in, which was walking the grounds of my winery, Lentari Cellars, with the foreman of my construction crew. What were they building? Well, that'd be one way-too-big-for-the-two-of-us mansion, from the ground up. My wife, Jillian, already owns her own house in town, but when we finally married, we had to sit down and decide what to do with the living arrangements.

We voted to live on the winery, which consists of fifty acres. We had the room, we had the funds, and we figured, why not? I signed the execution order for Bonnie Davies' old house, and surprised Jillian by presenting a set of house plans she had been drooling over ever since we first started looking.

This monster was going to have over seventy-five hundred feet of space. It included an indoor pool, a mini theater, a game room, a library, and a *secret* library that Jillian didn't know about. Yet. That's what I was doing today, finalizing the location of the access point to get to her secret hideaway.

"You can see here," the foreman was saying, referring to a large, rolled up set of blueprints he was holding open, "that we're on the ground floor now. This room here, to the right? That'll be a closet."

I whistled. The so-called closet looked like it was

bigger than my first apartment.

"Let me guess. This will be Jillian's, won't it?"

Chuck Whiteson, the guy trying to keep everyone organized with my construction project, nodded. "Yours will be back through there, in the hallway, on the left."

"Tiny in comparison?"

Chuck guided me over to a surprisingly large area.

"This is it right here. Not big enough for you?"

"Wow, I think it'll be fine," I assured him. "I don't own enough clothes to fill a space this size."

Chuck laughed and then indicated we should go through the doorway, into a room with a rounded opposite wall that I guessed to be the master suite.

"We are now directly above the game room. The reason I asked you here is that you had requested some type of access from this room to the one below, is that right?"

I nodded, and couldn't stop the grin from spreading on my face. Everyone always said I was nothing more than a big kid at heart. Well, they'd be right.

"Absolutely. Whatcha got for me?"

"I just wanted to know where you want it," Chuck clarified. "Whether here, in the main room, or through that doorway on the left, which is ... let me check the plans. Yes, here it is. That is a sitting room. Therefore, my question is, do you want your secret entrance to be in this room or *that* room?"

I looked back and forth between the master

suite and the sitting room.

"Phew, it's hard to decide," I admitted. "Logic suggests that I should move it away from where we're going to be sleeping, but I like the idea of a quick getaway, if needed. Hmm."

A few moments passed, in silence.

"We could always do both," Chuck slowly suggested, stifling a laugh.

My head jerked up. "Hey, I didn't think about that. Would that be too difficult to add?"

"You're paying the bills, Mr. Anderson. Anything is possible. You want both rooms to have a secret door? Both rooms it is."

"I like you," I said, giving him a grin.

Chuck smiled back. "I assume you're still wanting the rest of the modifications we talked about?"

"Oh, absolutely. I want this place just like Disneyland. Secret tunnels and doors everywhere. I want the full-on Clue mansion treatment."

Chuck tapped the rolled up plans.

"Got everything right here. We'll get working on it. Heads up, Mr. Anderson. I see Mrs. Anderson has just pulled into the driveway."

Together, we watched Jillian's SUV creep down the gravel road until her car was parked next to mine. She exited, walked to the passenger door behind the driver door, and opened it.

"There you go, guys. There's your daddy, right over there."

Two streaks of fur executed Superman jumps

from the car and sped toward me at Mach I. Barking like they thought they were driving off a pack of demons, both dogs arrived at my side and practically danced with joy as they wove around my legs. Watson even darted through a few times.

"They sure missed you," Chuck observed.

"You'd think I keep them in their kennels all waking moments of the day," I said, grinning.

Jillian arrived.

"Those were some mighty unhappy doggies, once they woke up from their nap and discovered you weren't there."

I shrugged. "They fell asleep on the couch. Who was I to wake them? I figured I'd let 'em sleep."

Chuck bade us farewell and headed toward a group of workers staring at a framed wall as though they had no inkling of what they should be doing next.

"How's everything going?" Jillian wanted to know. "Are we still on track for a spring completion date?"

"Probably late spring, but yeah, I think so."

"Will that include the landscaping?"

I let out a long sigh. "I wish. I'm treating the landscaping as Phase II. We have to wait for the house to be finished first. Trust me, I've tried to arrange it for everyone to be working at the same time, figuring it'll all be done that much sooner. Nope. You'd think I just suggested changing lead into gold."

Holding my wife's hand tightly in my own, we

walked a complete circle of our new house.

"It's much bigger than I realized," Jillian admitted.

"I was thinking the same thing. I've asked myself a few times just how much room two people could possibly need."

Jillian pointed at the corgis.

"Two people and two dogs, that is."

"True."

We were passing the rear of the house, with the Lentari Cellars' main processing building behind us, when we heard a shout. Turning, we noticed a lanky young man, with a full head of curly black hair, walking toward us, holding something red in his hand. I'm sorry to say I was frowning before my master vintner, Caden Burne, made it to within ten feet of us.

I held up my hands in a time-out, figuring Caden wanted to use my strong disdain for wine as a means of trying out a new recipe. Again.

"Hold your horses, pal. I don't have any soda with me."

Caden shook his head.

"I don't need you to try anything."

I relaxed almost immediately. "That's what I want to hear. What can we do for you?"

"Well, now that I think about it, I guess I *do* want you to try something for me."

The scowl was back.

"Right this second?" I warily asked.

Caden held up the red object he was holding.

"It's taken a few years for me to get the recipe right, and to be able to replicate the circumstances almost perfectly each time, but I finally did it. May I present our first bottle of Harvest Cheer? This is for you guys to try. And like, I hope."

Jillian was all smiles.

"Why thank you, my good sir. We can have this ... Zachary, stop scowling. You remember the sweet, dessert wine Caden proposed a year or two ago, don't you?"

"Oh, sure, I remember it," I confirmed, nodding my head. "That's the one made with moldy grapes. No thank you."

"Aww, come on, Zack," Caden pleaded. "You told me you actually liked it the last time you tried it."

"Tastes buds can change, can't they?" I argued.

"Not to that extent," Caden pointed out. He held the shimmery red bottle out to me. "Here, just take it. I ... scratch that. Jillian, I'm going to give this to you. You never know what'll happen to a bottle of wine if you place it in *his* hands."

"Too true," Jillian said. She took the bottle and held it up. "Oh, I love this! How did you get the sparkles in the glass? It's perfect for the holidays!"

"Isn't it?" Caden said, beaming. "I have a friend who's a glass-blower. He does some side jobs for several wineries. Consequently, he's a huge fan of our wine, Zack. Anyway, he says he's worked out a technique where he adds some crushed glass, coated with silver, into the mix. I couldn't begin to tell you how he does it, but he approached me with an example of a dessert wine bottle. I knew we had to have them as soon as I saw them."

"It's smaller than a normal wine bottle," I observed, holding the bottle up to the light. Sure enough, there were silver sparkles all throughout the bottle, from base to neck. "Wait. Didn't you say dessert wines are typically kept in smaller bottles?"

"Good job!" Caden praised. "You remembered!"

Grinning wildly, like a schoolboy who had just earned his first gold star of the day, I looked at Jillian. She was shaking her head.

"It helps distinguish them from the others," Caden was saying. "But, do you see here? And the neck there? The bottle's neck is elongated, which matches the bottle from our most well-known recipe. And that is …?"

"Oh, you're asking me again. Hold on. Our best seller? That'd be the Syrah, wouldn't it?"

"Correct again! Nicely done!"

"Don't make his head swell any bigger than it already has," Jillian giggled.

"All I ask is that you try it for me," Caden said, as he looked first at me, then at Jillian. "Have a good dinner, and then serve this. A standard pour of two ounces is more than enough."

"Two ounces?" I repeated. My smile was back. "Next time you should open with that."

"That's the standard amount," Caden told me. "Think about it. When you're served a dessert, isn't it usually a smaller portion?"

"Yeah, and I've always thought the restaurants were tightwads," I responded.

Caden sighed, looked at Jillian, and shook his head.

"He's *your* problem, Mrs. Anderson. I'm heading out."

"It's Friday," Jillian said. "Any big plans?"

"I ... I'm meeting someone," Caden admitted. "I haven't told anyone this, but I'm actually going on a blind date. Wish me luck!"

Jillian slipped her arm through mine.

"Always. Have a good time, Caden."

"Hope he has some good luck this time," I said. "I know he's tried dating a few times, and it never seems to work out for him."

"If this one crashes and burns, then I'll set him up with one of my single friends," Jillian promised. She checked the time on her watch. "Have you received any phone calls recently? Say, in the last hour or so?"

I pulled out my cell and checked the display. "No, I haven't. Should I have?"

"Well, I thought he would have called by now."

"Who?" I wanted to know.

Before my wife could answer, wouldn't you know it? My phone started ringing.

"This is the sort of thing that would've gotten you burned at the stake several hundred years ago," I said, smiling. "Hello, this is Zack. I'm sorry, hold on a second. You're *who*?" I looked at Jillian as I heard the name. "Yeah, it's been a while. Hold on a second. I'm going to put you on speaker."

"Who is it?" Jillian asked, trying to sound innocent.

I waggled a finger at her. "Don't play innocent with me, lady. It's precisely the person you thought it would be." I tapped a button on the display. "Director Hawk, it's nice to hear from you. How are things in Monterey Bay?"

Jonathan Hawk ran a tight ship at the Monterey Bay Aquarium, located in California. We got to know him when, during an attempted vacation, Jillian and I discovered a dead scuba diver floating in the ocean. We lent our help, discovered the aquarium had a subpar security system, and essentially made huge donations to them so they could upgrade their system.

We are now indefinite VIPs in their eyes, I suppose.

"We're all good here, Mr. Anderson. Mrs. Anderson, I assume you're listening?"

"I am."

"I'd like to say what a surprise this is, but I can't," I said. "So, what can we do for you, Mr. Hawk?"

"Jonathan, please. I hope I'm not intruding. After all, I know you're going over your house plans today."

Surprised, I looked at Jillian, who gave me a sheepish smile.

"We are, but we're done now. Can I ask how long ago you were talking to her?"

"Less than an hour. Such a lovely lady. You are

truly blessed to have her."

"Oh, I know it. The problem is, she knows it, too."

Jillian let out a laugh and smacked my arm.

"Don't rough him up too much," Jonathan instructed.

"No promises, Mr. Hawk. Er, Jonathan. I haven't really told Zachary about anything we discussed earlier. Perhaps you should start there?"

"Ah, got it. Mr. Anderson… er, Zack …you did us a tremendous favor by side-stepping our PR nightmare from a while back. I have a friend who runs her own facility and is experiencing, uh, her own setbacks. It's a brand new institution. She found her investors, lined up all her equipment, and is now just waiting on accreditation. For the record, they don't have it yet."

"From the sounds of it, they've got a difficult time waiting for them," Jillian said.

I took my wife's hand, gave it a few reassuring pats, and was about to turn back to my phone when I caught sight of the corgis. Both were now staring at my chest. Without realizing what I was doing, I sucked in my gut.

"If they don't get the help they need, then you're absolutely right," Jonathan confirmed. "Zack, have you heard of the CCCP?"

"The Central Committee of the Communist Party?" I incredulously asked. "She's Russian? I thought they didn't call themselves that anymore. Where the hell does your friend work? Moscow?"

We heard a snort on the phone, followed immediately by a round of guttural coughing, as if our aquarium friend's drink just went down the wrong tube.

"Are you okay?" Jillian asked, concerned.

A few more coughs sounded.

"Wow, I did not see that coming," Jonathan admitted. "Zack, that's one very active imagination you've got. The CCCP I'm referring to is the Caesar Colony Center for Penguins. Communists. I just snorted my coffee and now I need to change my shirt."

"If this is as brand new of an institution as you say, then I'd start off by choosing a completely different name," I said.

"I assure you, the name of her facility is the *last* thing on her mind," Dr. Hawk said, his voice turning grim. "Although, now that I think about it, I'm thinking she probably chose that name on purpose."

"Penguins, huh?" I repeated, and started to nod when I felt myself frowning. Penguins? "I know you're not suggesting we go to the South Pole."

"I don't expect anything of the sort," Jonathan confirmed.

"Whew, that's good to hear. Can you imagine that? Tying Sherlock and Watson to a sled and telling 'em *mush*. What a visual that would make."

Sherlock let out a snort, followed by Watson shaking her collar for nearly ten seconds straight. I was watching my little girl make one heck of a racket when my eyes settled on my shirt. It just so happened to be one of the souvenirs I'd picked up during our first cruise. Was that why the dogs were staring earlier? Alaska? They thought I'd be willing to go to Alaska? At the tail end of fall?

"Zachary's eyes just confirmed what you haven't told him yet," Jillian reported. "Namely, *where* the CCCP is located."

"Sitka, Alaska," Jonathan confirmed.

I turned to Jillian and pointed at my shirt.

"I think that explains why the dogs were looking at my shirt earlier."

"You're wearing one of your Alaska shirts? Today, of all days? How bizarre!"

"You're wearing a shirt that says Alaska on it?" Jonathan asked. "And your dogs stared at you, like they did for those life preservers?"

During our visit to the Monterey Bay Aquarium, the dogs were asked to find a missing journal. Needless to say, they found it. Jonathan wasn't kidding when he claimed he knew how the dogs worked.

"They did. Wait a moment. I didn't think there were indigenous penguins living in the Arctic."

"There *aren't*," Jonathan confirmed. "But, that doesn't mean they can't set up shop in a similar climate."

"Tell him what type of penguins they are," Jillian suggested.

"Emperors," Jonathan answered. "And if you didn't know, they are one of the largest species of penguins on the planet. Adults can get up to four feet tall, and weigh fifty pounds."

"I'm sorry for asking, but are they endangered?" I asked.

"There's less than a handful of fully accredited breeding facilities in existence," I was told. "The answer to your question is *very*. Marianne's work is … I'm sorry. Marianne Rozhkov is the most determined woman you will ever meet. She's young, too, for one so ambitious. The fact that she turned to me for help tells me she's stuck between a rock and a hard place."

"She heard about what we did for you guys, is that it?" I asked.

"She heard about Sherlock and Watson's role in the recovery of some very old stolen merchandise."

"Irish merchandise," Jillian guessed, offering me a smile.

"Exactly," Jonathan said. "So, Zack, would you be willing to grant me a second favor and see what you and your wonderful dogs might be able to do for my colleague?"

I looked at my wife for confirmation. Jillian nodded and took my hand.

"We're in," I told our friend. "What can we do? What kind of problems is CCCP having?"

"Aside from minor technical issues, which they can contend with, there's just one that they're worried about. If it isn't resolved by the time the inspector gets there, then they'll fail their accreditation and would essentially have to close."

"What's the problem?" I asked again. A nagging voice in the back of my mind was telling me I wasn't going to like the answer.

"They were successful," Jonathan announced. "CCCP's first attempt at incubating a viable egg produced six possibilities. I'm very pleased to say that one hatched."

"That's wonderful!" Jillian exclaimed.

"Not really. The chick was stolen."

TWO

D idn't you tell me that you've been here before? I thought you said you liked Sitka!"

I pointed at the falling snow, visible through the windows of their tiny, regional airport. But, before I could even start complaining about the weather, I caught sight of the plane that flew us in and my arm automatically swiveled in that direction.

"Let's not forget the puddle jumper that flew us from Juneau. I don't think I've ever been in both a window seat *and* an aisle seat at the same time."

"The dogs sure loved it. Didn't you? Oh, you two were so well behaved on the plane! You made us proud, Sherlock! You, too, Watson!"

Having been forewarned that Sitka's snowy season was due to start in less than a fortnight, which explained why the inspector chose to fly in before the middle of November, the two of us adjusted our heavy winter coats. I felt a tug on Sherlock's leash. Glancing down, I saw that both he and Watson were staring at the airport's one and only luggage carousel. Moments later, a cherry light set into the ceiling began flashing. With a loud, grating rumble, the carousel was set into motion. Ten minutes later, bags began to appear.

"Mr. and Mrs. Anderson! Oh, thank *goodness*! I thought I might've missed you!"

Sherlock and Watson turned to face the newcomer and let loose a few warning woofs, which had the intended effect of making the college-age lady come to an immediate halt. She was short, with long blond hair pulled into a low pony-tail, and was wearing a thick winter coat, a bright blue scarf, black earmuffs, and snow boots. She smiled warmly at the dogs, took her earmuffs off, and offered me her hand.

"I'm Shannon. Shannon Silverman. I'm Dr. Rozhkov's assistant. I'm so sorry I'm late. Looks like winter is anxious to put in an appearance, doesn't it? Oh! I've been waiting for this! You two are Sherlock and Watson, aren't you?"

"They are," I confirmed.

The woofs vanished in the blink of an eye. Both dogs dropped their guarded stance and raced each other to see who could make it to the stranger first. Thankfully, they didn't have far to go.

Sherlock arrived first and reared up on his hind legs. Watson wove between the girl's legs, panting excitedly. Less than two seconds later, both were on their backs and staring at Shannon with hopeful eyes.

"Sherlock, Watson, how about showing a little modesty, huh?" I was ignored. "He hasn't done that to me in a while," I grumped. I heard Jillian laughing behind me. "What? What's so funny?"

"They're not paying attention to you because Shannon came prepared. Look at them. She's giving them doggie treats."

Once the corgis were crunching away on their biscuits, Shannon straightened.

"For your convenience, I've been assigned to you guys as your liaison for the duration of your visit. If there's anything you need, anything at all, I humbly ask that, er, you ask, I guess."

"How far away is CCCP?" I asked.

I had just noticed the arrival of one of our suitcases and hurried over to retrieve it. Looking back, I really don't know why I was in a hurry. There had been only one other couple on the plane, and they already claimed a piece of their luggage, too.

"It's about twenty minutes away. I've got one of the company vans parked outside, so once you have your bags, all you'll have to do is to follow me."

Our little procession followed our guide toward the main exit. The doors slid open and the cold blast of arctic air stopped me in my tracks. Looking down at the dogs, I briefly wondered if I should take the time to put the dogs' coats on. Yes, I know they'd probably be fine, since both have thick coats and undercoats, but hey, this is Alaska, and that white stuff falling from the sky meant it was in the very low thirties out there. It's cold for a reason.

"We'll put them on once we get inside the van," Jillian promised, correctly guessing what I was thinking.

Once all of our luggage had been stored, and the four of us were safe and snug in the idling vehicle, Shannon guided the van north, past the city limits and eventually turned right to head up a surprisingly steep street.

"Is this safe?" my wife asked, as she belted the long, thick wool sweater in place around Watson's tummy.

"All of our vehicles are equipped with four-wheel drive," Shannon explained. "Plus, you just don't go that fast. It doesn't matter what you drive, or how powerful the engine is, or even how big the tires are. If you don't respect the road, then it'll waste no time reminding you who's really in charge."

"Are there really no roads leading out of the city?" Jillian asked.

I looked up. I hadn't heard *that* particular piece of trivia before.

"Really? You guys can't drive to another city? You're cut off from the rest of civilization?"

"The only way in or out is by boat or airplane," Shannon confirmed. "All of our supplies have to be shipped in. That's why everything is so expensive."

"Everything?" I asked, amazed. "Gasoline? Groceries? Drinking water? Salt for the roads?"

"Everything," Shannon said, nodding. "If you prefer your isolation, then Sitka is the place to be."

The road we were following suddenly veered right, away from the water and the town. Trees loomed over us. Thankfully, most of them didn't have that much snow on them. Yet.

"How much snow do you get here?" I asked.

"Like any place, it varies," Shannon answered. "On average, though, I'd say we get somewhere around five."

"Inches? That's not so bad. I thought it'd be more."

"Feet," Shannon corrected. "Five *feet* of snow."

"Yikes," I breathed. "You guys must really like your snow."

I felt the road's incline lessen. We were nearing the top of whatever ridge we had been ascending.

"As far as quantities of snow, Sitka really isn't too bad," Shannon was saying, as the road we were on leveled off and headed east. "You want to talk about a lot of snow? Head to Skagway. They can easily double what we get."

"Holy crap on a cracker, that's a lot of snow," I whistled.

Both dogs suddenly scrambled to their feet. Sherlock hurried to my side and reared up to put his front legs on my lap, which usually meant he wanted to be picked up.

"What is it?" I asked, as I hooked my fingers under his squat, muscular legs, and lifted. "There's really not much to see here, so ..."

"*Woof.*"

Watson whined and then decided, since no one

was giving her the same treatment, to mimic her packmate. Jillian set her on her lap and was ready to give her some friendly scratches, but was promptly ignored. The little red and white corgi leaned over to the window, looked left, and finally right, and whined again.

"What's gotten into them?" I wondered aloud.

"WOOF!" Sherlock repeated, with a little more force.

That was when I felt the van slow.

"Are we there?" I asked. Sherlock, for being such a small dog, and a very manageable twenty-nine pounds, had the ability to triple his weight whenever he chose to put all his weight on one paw. That's what he did for me as he fidgeted on my lap. "Oof, keep that up and I'm gonna put you on a diet, pal."

"Ooooo!" Watson howled.

The van came to a gentle stop.

"What's going on?" Jillian asked.

Looking through the open windows revealed a surprise. Standing defensively in the middle of the street, daring us to try and force her to move, was a mother moose. Directly behind her was a small, young calf.

I gave Sherlock a healthy scratch behind his ears.

"Hey, pal. That's someone you don't want to tangle with. I'll bet she could drop kick you well into next week. Leave these guys alone, okay? Wh-what are you doing?"

Jillian glanced at me. "Sherlock is sitting? Why

is he sitting on your lap?"

I pointed at Watson. "Hey, she's doing the same thing. Shannon? Can we not go around them?"

"And risk scaring the baby? No, I'm sorry. We're going to have to wait for … oh, they're moving off. You're in luck! I've had a mother moose literally lay in the middle of the street before and not move for nearly two hours."

Jillian nudged my shoulder and pointed at the moose.

"Maybe you should be taking a picture?"

"Hmm? Oh, uh, okay. You're suggesting Sherlock and Watson think this is a corgi clue?"

"A corgi clue?" Shannon repeated, from the driver's seat. "I have to ask. What is that?"

"Whenever we're working a case," I explained, "and the dogs fixate on something, I'll usually take a picture of whatever it is so that we can check them out at a later date."

"How would a moose family pertain to a missing penguin chick?" Shannon asked.

"No idea," I admitted. "Then again, we could be misreading this and the corgis might just be reacting to their first ever encounter with a moose."

Shannon's eyes were watching me in the rearview mirror.

"How would you know?"

I held up my phone. "Watch. After I take this picture, either the dogs will sit up and act like nothing's happened, or else they'll probably continue to stare at mama moose there."

I took two snapshots. Both dogs immediately rose to their feet and returned to the spot where they had been laying, next to our suitcases.

"Corgi clue it is," I announced.

"But … a moose?" Shannon reiterated, clearly confused. "I don't see how it could be important."

"You will by the time this is over," I promised.

"Shannon, may I ask a question?"

Our liaison looked at my wife and nodded. "Go ahead, Mrs. Anderson."

"Where will we be staying? We were assured that accommodations would be provided. Are they near the facility?"

"We've booked you a wonderful cabin in downtown Sitka. Two bedrooms, wood fireplace, kitchenette, everything you need has been provided. Once Ms. Rozhkov has had a chance to meet with you and give you a tour, then I'll be taking you back to town so you have a chance to settle in."

My wife nodded, pleased.

"Thank you."

Unsure how I should formulate my next question, I cleared my throat. Suddenly, I had every set of eyeballs in the van locked on me.

"Umm, Shannon? I'm sorry, I've got to ask something. Your CEO, Ms. Rozhkov? Based on the name, I'm guessing she's Russian?"

"Yes, although you'd never be able to tell by listening to her. That's not a problem, is it?"

CASE OF THE UNLUCKY EMPEROR

"Oh, no, not at all. It's just that ... well, a Russian CEO chooses to name her facility CCCP?"

Our driver burst out in giggles.

"You wouldn't be the first to ask that. She insists it wasn't intentional. And even though she has a Russian name, she was born in Washington."

"Oh?" Jillian asked. "Do you know where? I know a lot of people up there."

"A small little town called Steilacoom. It's a suburb of Tacoma."

My wife nodded. "I do know of the area. A good friend of mine has a son who attends Steilacoom High School."

"Does Dr. Rozhkov speak Russian?" I asked.

Shannon laughed. "Not a word, I'm afraid."

"And Emperor penguins?" I continued. "In the Arctic?"

Shannon continued to laugh, pausing only long enough to fetch a tissue from a small pack sitting on the console between seats.

"Again, not the first time I've heard that. Do you know how many times I've walked by Ms. Rozhkov's office and heard her stating she's well aware there are no penguins this far north? Dozens and dozens of times."

"I look forward to meeting her," Jillian said, taking my hand in hers.

"We're nearly there," Shannon announced. "If you look ahead, you'll see the break in the trees about a mile in front of us. On the other side of the tree line is our facility."

"How big is it?" I asked, once the main complex came into view.

"Doesn't look that big, does it?" Shannon admitted. She pressed a button on what looked like a garage door opener and waited for a chain link gate to roll open. "We have about forty-five hundred feet of space, with just over ten acres at our disposal."

"Ten acres?" I repeated, surprised. "For penguins?"

"These are Emperors," Shannon clarified. "They can get pretty big. We want to make sure they don't feel crowded. This property started with less than half an acre, but Dr. Rozhkov was able to talk the city into selling some of the surrounding land."

"How many penguins call this place home?" I asked.

"As it is, we only have sixteen breeding pairs right now, separated into two colonies. The Woody colony has ten, and Buzz has six. There's a third yard, but it's much smaller. The purpose was to have a place to separate a pair if necessary. Thankfully, we haven't had to use it yet."

"Do the penguins really need that much room or are you planning on bringing in more pairs?" Jillian asked.

"We have the facility to accommodate up to two-hundred breeding pairs. We just have to prove proof of concept first. I'll let Dr. Rozhkov go over the details. And here we are. In fact, there's Ms. Rozhkov now. She's waiting for us."

The van pulled to a stop at the top end of a circular driveway. A light dusting of snow had fallen, turning everything white. The nearby trees were picture postcard perfect, and CCCP's large main complex strongly resembled an oversized Victorian manor. In fact, I had to look twice. The roof had a number of steep gables. There was a tower on the northern wall, and of the three buildings that comprised the facility, there was a dormer on each wall, facing each direction. Some had two, actually. Decorative woodwork was evident in the large porch wrapping the front entrance, and worked its way up, to the second story.

"That has to be the prettiest animal facility I have ever seen," Jillian said, awed.

"It's just a remodeled house," Shannon informed us. I helped her unload our luggage from the van. "It was significantly cheaper to remodel an existing structure than build one from scratch. Thankfully, this mansion was on the market for less than half what it originally cost."

"We got it for a steal," a new voice agreed.

We turned to see a woman in her late thirties approach. She was the same height as Jillian, which made her five-foot six, and had shoulder-length brunette hair. She was wearing a thick, padded winter coat, black slacks, earmuffs, and dark gloves. She pulled one off and held out a hand.

"Dr. Marianne Rozhkov. I'm so very pleased to meet you."

"Zack Anderson," I said, taking her hand. Shannon was right. Dr. Rozhkov didn't have any trace of a Russian accent. "This is my wife, Jillian. And, of course, we mustn't forget Sherlock and Watson."

"They are so cute!"

Marianne reached down to give each corgi a pat on the head.

"Come, it's freezing out here. Let's go inside."

We thanked Shannon for the ride and, with me holding both suitcases and Jillian manning the leashes, followed Marianne up the porch steps into the house.

The first thing we noticed was that the interior had been completely remodeled. It may look like a residence from the outside, but the similarities ended there. As soon as you stepped inside, you'd know you were *not* in someone's home.

I could smell antiseptic scents in the air. Strong chemicals, likely used to clean and sanitize equipment, were prevalent. What used to be the house's foyer had now joined with the main living room and was a communal sitting area. Several armchairs were arranged in a large semi-circle and were set around a lit fireplace. Wood crackled as it burned, casting off a very welcoming warmth. Both corgis approached and promptly shook themselves off.

Marianne held out a hand.

"Let me take your coats. They'll be hung there, in that closet. Just leave your luggage. No one will bother it. Did Shannon tell you she'll be taking you to the cabin we rented for you? Good. All right, can I give you a tour?"

I held out a hand. "Please do. You lead the way and we'll follow."

With me in possession of both leashes once more, we followed Marianne as she moved deeper into the house. We slowed at a white circular staircase.

"Offices are all upstairs. Will you be needing a place to work?"

I pointed at the dogs. "They don't really work that way. We need to be able to look around. Once we, meaning *they*, find something, they'll let me know. Whether or not anyone can make the connection remains to be seen."

Marianne regarded us for a few moments.

"Is that how they did it in Monterey?"

I nodded. "Yep. They found a missing log book when no one else knew where to begin looking. They've located missing jewelry, sculptures, and even people. I don't know how they do it, but they never fail. It continues to amaze me."

"Very well. Let's keep moving. Through here is the kitchen, with our storage freezers. All of our penguins' diets are created here. That freezer there —I won't even begin to tell you how much that walk-in unit cost. Over there, we have two smaller backup units we can use should this one fail."

We moved past the kitchen and veered right.

"Through there is where we conduct

examinations. There are three fully stocked exam rooms, and should we need a fourth, our surgery room can also double as another room."

"Do you let the birds incubate their own eggs, or do you collect them to bring in here?" Jillian wanted to know.

In response, Marianne pointed at a large glass box with a heavy lid. Inside, thanks to a number of bright lights, we saw several rows of pear-shaped objects that were of a greenish-white color. Each of the eggs were about five inches long, and around three inches wide.

"How freakin' cool," I said, although it wasn't directed to anyone other than myself.

"I wish I could share your enthusiasm," Marianne quietly told us.

"Worried about the chick?" I asked, looking up. "If there's any chance of recovering that baby penguin, those two will be the ones to do it."

"I certainly hope so, Mr. Anderson. As you can see, none of the other viables have hatched. We're going to give this batch more time, of course, but this represents our first attempt. We were very much hoping we'd be able to make a press release, proclaiming our first attempt had been successful. However, I'm now thinking that's not going to happen."

"Your first attempt *has* been successful," Jillian corrected. "The missing chick is proof of that. Clearly, someone doesn't want you, or this facility, to succeed."

"You don't think we've already considered that?" Marianne asked, dropping her voice even lower. "The only way something like this could've been pulled off is to have inside help. That's what keeps me awake at night."

The dogs rose to their feet, shook their collars, and looked at the closest window. Catching sight of the dogs, Marianne nodded.

"You're right. We should continue with the tour. Follow me, and I'll show you our medical facilities."

Dr. Rozhkov walked past us and through a door on the left. She turned right, and we were back in the kitchen. She pulled a set of keys from her jacket pocket and unlocked a door that looked like it was nothing more than a closet. Or a pantry.

It was neither.

We were looking at a wide, refreshingly clean staircase heading down. Once the lights were activated, we could see that it was only nine or ten steps down, before depositing us into a converted basement. White tile was everywhere: floors, walls, and countertops. The wall to my right held four large, metal sinks. Locked storage cabinets lined the wall on my left. Directly in front, I could see several white tables, currently folded up and secured against the wall. And on the wall behind me were more freezers. Three huge chest freezers lined the far wall. You know the kind. The ones big enough to hide a body? Those ones.

I know, it's morbid, but hey, it's how my mind

works.

Continuing my scan of the room, I looked down and saw the room had no fewer than five different drains.

Something dangling from the ceiling caught my eye. Looking up, I saw a coiled rubber hose and a metal arm which would allow it to swing out over the room. It reminded me of the stalls for washing your own car. Smiling, I realized why the room had been set up in this manner.

"Necropsies," I said. "Although, I can't imagine why you'd need so much space."

Marianne regarded me with a smile and a nod.

"Not many people know that word. Nicely done."

I shrugged. "Hey, what can I say? I'm a writer. I got some major negative feedback from the fans about it, but I did have one book that dealt with a mysterious rash of animal deaths. Thought it'd be prudent to look up the proper term."

"Everything you need to run a professional animal hospital can be found in this room," Dr. Rozhkov explained. "We call this the Infirmary. We're fairly remote here, so we needed to be certain we weren't lacking for anything."

"What's through there?" Jillian asked, pointing at the large double doors facing north.

"The way to our yards. We need to go back upstairs before we head outside. The snow has picked up and is getting heavier."

"Do we really have to?" Jillian asked, worried.

"I'd be more than happy to take your word for it."

Marianne snapped her fingers. "I know what we can do. If you'll come with me, I'll show you how we can finish the tour the easy way."

"I'm all for that," I said, grinning.

Five minutes later, we were seated at a console that I thought looked straight out of Jurassic Park. There were video screens everywhere. Banks of controls, digital displays, and computers covered every square inch of counter space and the main wall.

"Wow, all of this for your penguins?" I asked, amazed.

"This is our control center. From here, we can monitor every animal under our care, whether they're out in the yards, or in their pens. We can monitor the weather over all ten acres at our disposal. There are cameras in the incubation room, food prep, hospital, and all throughout the three yards."

Dr. Rozhkov pressed a button on the controls. The entire panel of security feeds went dark, turning into one giant black screen. Then, a new feed appeared. We were looking at a picture of an exterior exhibit, complete with a small lake. White artificial structures had been erected, made to resemble the ice formations found in Antarctica.

"Where are they at?" I asked, leaning forward. "I can't see anything in there."

"Woody and Buzz are both safe and secure in their interior kennels," Marianne reported. "I'm sorry. I'm talking about our two colonies, by the way. Once the storm passes, and it's deemed safe for the animals, we'll then open the outer doors and let them out to explore."

"Woody and Buzz?" I repeated. "We heard that before. Are those code names for your flocks? Uh, herds? What do you call a group of penguins?"

"It depends on what they're doing," Marianne answered. "If they're swimming, then it's a *raft*."

"Just like the otters," I said, turning to Jillian.

Dr. Rozhkov nodded. "Precisely. When the penguins are on land and walking, it's *waddle*."

"A waddle," I snorted, laughing.

"A collective term you could use, if you just wanted to refer to a number of penguins, would be a *colony*, or maybe even a *rookery*."

"A colony," Jillian repeated. "This is the Caesar Center Colony for Penguins, isn't it? The CCCP?"

"You're going to ask me about the acronym, aren't you? Well, what can I say? I wanted to come up with something that people wouldn't forget."

"It definitely worked," I confirmed. "It made me look twice."

Marianne pointed at the screen. "In case you're wondering, there are ten breeding pairs in Woody, and six in Buzz. We have two exhibits that are four acres each. Woody and Buzz each have their own areas."

"Do they need that much room?" Jillian asked.

"Those yards can each handle up to a hundred breeding pairs. We planned ahead."

"What about the third?" I asked. "I thought there's another smaller pen?"

"Yes. In case we need to separate one or more birds away from the others, we have a small, half-acre enclosure that can be used. It's currently empty."

CCCP's director sighed and pressed a few buttons on her console. The display darkened a second time, and when it brightened, it was back to the grid with the multiple views. She slowly spun in her chair until she was facing the four of us. Well, make that *two*. Both dogs had settled to the floor and had their heads resting on their paws. Their eyes were closed and were softly snoring.

"Jet lag," I said, by way of explanation.

"I'm sorry to drag you up here like this. I was desperate. I didn't know what else to do."

"Tell us what happened," Jillian suggested.

"Two days ago, one of the eggs hatched, and we had our very first captive-born bird. We were all ecstatic. This was our very first attempt! No breeding center has ever been able to produce results this quickly."

"How many are there?" I asked. "Penguin centers, that is."

"There are a number of breeding facilities," Dr. Rozhkov told us. "However, less than a handful deal with Emperor penguins. They are notoriously difficult to breed in captivity. For some reason, the eggs never hatch. We don't know what is happening to the eggs, only that something causes them to simply remain unhatched."

"Go on," Jillian urged.

"Yesterday," Marianne continued, "our swing keeper was making her rounds, checking the colonies, the incubator, and so on, when she noticed the chick was missing. She assumed the baby had been returned to the parents, but no, it hadn't. Alarmed, she got on the phone and woke everyone up."

"No one knew anything about the chick, did they?" I asked.

"Not a word. You see the system we have here. Cameras cover *everything*, yet when I went to check the footage, it doesn't show a thing. There are no gaps in the footage and there are no after-hour access in the logs. The security footage confirms no one else was on the premises, yet somehow, our chick has disappeared."

"I hate to say this," I began, "but have you considered it could've fallen victim to a predator?"

"I don't think it was kept outside," Jillian told me.

"It wasn't," Marianne confirmed. "That's why you're here. This couldn't have come at a more inopportune time. As you probably know, we haven't received our accreditation yet. The inspector will be here in four days. If we don't have that chick back here in that time, or else have a viable, plausible explanation why it disappeared in the first place, then we're going to get shut down.

"Mr. Anderson. Mrs. Anderson. You need to

know that I used every favor, every trick in the trade I could think of to get this place created. I, myself, worked in the animal husbandry field for over twenty years. I've used my own contacts, and former acquaintances, to secure our birds. I'm the one who found the investors. I'm the one who invested every last penny I had into this place. We *need* to be accredited by the fifteenth of this month. And, this being Alaska, I can tell you that winter usually sets in on the eighteenth, plus or minus a day or two. The inspector will be here in four short days. I can't stall him, and I obviously can't put the weather on hold. These dates are firm, and there's nothing I can do about it."

I pointed at the two snoozing corgis.

"Well, Doc, you came to the right place. Those two sleeping beauties may not look like it, but they are absolute experts in locating that which doesn't want to be found. We're on the case."

Dr. Rozhkov's eyes filled.

"Thank you. Thank you so much."

Jillian reached into her purse and offered Marianne a tissue.

"Again, thank you. So, if you don't mind me asking, how does this work? I asked Jonathan Hawk that question, and the only thing he could tell me is that he has absolute faith in your two dogs."

"Well, what we'll do, starting tomorrow, is investigate the area. It means that I'll let Sherlock and Watson take the lead and see if anything catches their attention. When something inevitably does, then I'll take a picture and note what we're looking at, and then sit down to review the pictures later."

"Where it'll make sense?" Marianne asked.

"Hopefully. Usually, the dogs point us in the right direction," Jillian explained. "So, that means we'll probably look around the complex, and might even go back to town and see if there's anything there."

"It's an inside job," Marianne insisted. "I just know it. The chick *must* be here somewhere."

"And if it isn't, then it'd be good to expand the search from the start," I said.

"You impressed Jonathan," Dr. Rozhkov recalled. "And I know from experience he doesn't impress easily. Do what you need to do. I'll give you access to every square inch of this facility. If there's something here, then I want to …"

"*Woof.*"

As one, Jillian, Dr. Rozhkov and I looked down at the dogs. The last time I personally checked on them, which was about five minutes ago, both appeared to be sleeping. Now? They were awake and standing up.

"When did you guys wake up?" I asked, surprised. "Whatever. What's up, guys? Do you smell something?"

Jillian handed me the leashes and watched as I was led by them to the opposite wall, which had a row of open bookcases. Sherlock was sniffing along the ground. Watson watched for a few moments before her nose lowered and she, too, was checking the floor.

"Are they giving us an example of how they work?" Marianne asked, smiling. "That was thoughtful of them."

I frowned and shook my head. "Oh, they're smart, that's for sure, but I don't think this is … heads up. We're headed out of the room."

"What now?" I heard Marianne ask my wife.

"We follow," Jillian answered.

Sherlock and Watson, with their noses glued to the floor, led us to the stairs and back to the ground floor. They then retraced their steps, taking us back to the front door, only they veered to the left. Sherlock promptly sat in front of the door.

"What's in there?" I quietly asked.

"It's just a closet," Marianne answered. She stepped forward to open the door and showed us. "There's nothing in here but our coats."

Sherlock was back on his feet. He stepped forward and nudged Jillian's scarf, which had been wrapped around her coat. He then turned to look at us.

"He wants us to go outside," I translated. "Really, pal? It's snowing out there. It's cold. We really don't want to …"

"Awwwoooowooooowoooo."

It was probably one of Sherlock's lowest howls yet. Actually, it sounded more argumentative than conversational.

Sighing, I pulled my coat free and put it on. Looking over at my wife, I gave her a questioning look. Jillian nodded and took her coat from my outstretched hand.

"I'll go get mine," Dr. Rozhkov said. "This is something I want to see."

Once we were all prepared, with the dogs wearing their coats, too, we were guided through the house to a door I had noticed earlier. Turned out it was the door you'd take if you wanted to exit the facility and head toward the penguin yards from the main floor. A second building was directly before us. Smaller than the main house, this one was not quite as ornately decorated as the first, but it still matched the other. We hurried up to the secondary building's main entrance and waited for the good doctor to unlock the door.

A thick, protective flap was lifted and I watched Dr. Rozhkov punch in a code, then insert a key into the door. We were quickly ushered inside, since the snowfall had picked up and had already accumulated an extra two inches in the last hour. We kicked the snow off our shoes and turned to Marianne, anxious to see if she'd be willing to give us an explanation of where we were, and what we were looking at.

Instead, both dogs gave themselves a thorough shaking and pulled us past the meticulously spotless metal tables, acres of countertops, sinks, and shelves of non-perishable food items. I could see huge bottles of vitamins, vials of liquids, and trays of various implements.

We finally stopped at a wall that had only one door on it. It was large, made of solid steel, and had a big number two on it. Was this a door to the second penguin yard?

Marianne unlocked the door and we stepped outside, into the exhibit.

"Don't worry. The penguins are all indoors right now and none of them congregate this far away from their kennels. Even so, we should limit how long we're out here."

For the record, I'll say it didn't take long. The two corgis made it about twenty steps inside before they stopped at a six-foot-tall cast iron lamp post.

"It's just a lamp," Marianne was saying. "It kicks on automatically, after sunset. Is this all they wanted to look at? We should … Mr. Anderson, why did they just sit?"

I studied the corgis. Both were sitting by the base of the lamp post. Sherlock, however, was giving me a look that said he hoped I figured it out soon, 'cause he wasn't enjoying himself in this cold weather. Thankfully, it didn't take me long.

The lamp post was modeled after the old fashioned street lamps from the turn of the century. This one was perfectly symmetrical, in that the top split into two gently-curved arcs, each tipped with a glass-covered light. However, the longer I stared at the post, the more I realized it wasn't quite symmetrical after all. At the junction where the two light arms split apart, there was a small, cylindrical object that looked like a black stogie. It had been placed on the back of the post, as if to better hide it from prying eyes.

I reached up and, with a little effort, pulled the object loose. I turned to look at Marianne and I held it up.

"Tell me, Doc. Is this one of your cameras?"

She shook her head.

THREE

Our cabin was quiet the following morning. The log fire that had been lit the previous evening had been stoked for the night, but had long since gone out. Thankfully, the small cabin's powerful gas furnace kept the interior temperature from getting too cold.

Inside the two bedroom, one bathroom structure, no one was moving around. Yet. The king bed had several fluffy quilts covering the occupants, but that wasn't the reason husband and wife were uncomfortable. Two lumps on the bed, stretched horizontally rather than vertically, lay unmoving, in the direct center, and refused to be moved.

"Freaking bed hogs. Come on, share, would you?" I heard a giggle come from Jillian's direction. "Laugh it up, Chuckles. I can see you're teetering on the edge, just like I am."

"Turn up the thermostat, would you? I'm not getting out of bed until it's at least ten degrees warmer."

"Ten, huh? Sure you're not overexaggerating?"

"You need to get the heat going before I put a single toe outside of this bed," Jillian told me. "I assume you'd like my help today? Well, if you want it, you'd better plan on making it warmer in here. Just look at that floor. I swear I see ice on it."

"I'll get your skates, my dear."

"Ha ha. Will you start a fire?"

I looked over at the wood-burning fireplace.

"Probably not. If we were going to be staying here for a while, then yes, I would. However, Shannon will be here to pick us up in … what time is it, anyway? Feels like three in the morning."

"It's 6:30, Zachary."

Both corgis, practically invisible amidst the folds of the thick comforters, lazily stretched, rolled, and promptly went back to sleep. Little boogers. How I'd love to do the same.

Once I had the furnace going, and the interior of the cabin was a very toasty seventy degrees, we *officially* started our day. Jillian headed for the shower, and I took the dogs outside.

"Would you guys hurry up?" I demanded, as we made our way down the yet-to-be-shoveled sidewalk. "Just find a spot and go. In case you haven't figured it out yet, it's freezing out here, and I don't have a nice, thick coat like you two."

Sherlock stopped at a snow-covered bush and

moments later, I saw wisps of steam rising up. Well, that was one way to know whether or not the dogs were done. Watson did her business, and as we headed back to the cabin, I looked up to study the dull gray sky. I couldn't see any individual clouds, but rather a thick gray mass above our heads. I lived in Idaho long enough to recognize more snow clouds when I see them. I mentally crossed my fingers that the heavy snowfall hadn't decided to start early this year. After all, if neither boat nor plane could manage a safe arrival or departure, we wouldn't be going anywhere until spring of next year.

"*Rrrrrrr.*"

I was so shocked I stopped in my tracks. Sherlock, too. Since when did Watson—and only Watson—growl at something? I immediately stooped and put an arm around her.

"What's the matter? What are you growling at?"

Sherlock nudged my other arm. There I was, wearing sweats, a t-shirt, and sweatshirt, squatting in the snow with an arm around each of my dogs. I might as well have been wearing a shirt with *tourist* labeled on the back.

"*Ooooo,*" Watson howled.

That was about the time the rest of me woke up and took note of my surroundings. There, placed in front of the trees on the left of our little cabin, was a dragon. Don't get me wrong, it was obviously not a real one, but some type of metallic, made-from-junk sculpture. Like our surroundings, it also was covered by several inches of snow. How I missed walking by that thing several times last night was beyond me.

"*Woof.*"

Looks like Sherlock finally noticed the sculpture, too. Both he and Watson had plunked their butts on the snow-covered sidewalk and were staring straight at the dragon. I had to give the leash a small tug to get their attention.

"It's just a sculpture. Let's go, okay? It's not real."

Neither dog moved.

Sighing, I pulled out my phone and snapped a picture. Both dogs immediately rose and trotted in front of me, as though they were personally responsible for saving the town of Sitka from a huge fire-breathing reptile.

Back inside the cabin, we breakfasted, rehashed the events of yesterday, and prepared our things for our trip back to CCCP.

"We can now add dragons to the list, next to the moose we saw earlier," I reported, as we gathered our belongings.

Jillian looked up. "Did I hear that right? Dragons?"

"There's a metal dragon sculpture just over there, sitting among the trees. Watson saw it first and started growling. Cutest damn growl I've ever heard."

"Huh. All right. One dragon. Got it. Let me ask you something. Do you think they'll have figured out who placed that camera outside one of their exhibits?"

I polished off my orange juice and noticed Jillian had slid the remainder of hers over to me. I drained the glass and then nodded.

"I would think so. Movies and television shows make it sound so simple. Apparently, there's some clever way to get the device to tell you *where* the information it collects is sent. Once you have an IP address, then the rest is history."

"Think it'll be that easy?"

"Knowing our luck, the answer is no."

There was a knock on the door. I cringed, expecting to hear both dogs go ballistic. After all, anyone who knocks—or rings the doorbell—back home is clearly a secret assassin and must be outed *immediately*. But, did they do that this time? No.

"I'll never figure you two out," I said, as I pulled the door open. "Hi, Shannon. We're ready here. Let me get the bags and we'll get going."

Shannon smiled brightly and nodded.

"Sounds good, Mr. Anderson."

"Please. It's Zack."

"Okay, Zack. I'll be waiting in the van."

We had just turned left, onto Halibut Point Road, when both Sherlock and Watson scrambled to their feet. Figures. They had just settled down from their encounter with the dragon after we drove by it.

"What now?" I asked, as I turned to look in the back seat. Both dogs were glued to the window behind Jillian, staring out. "They're looking right," I reported. "What's ...? Oh, you've got to be kidding. Well, I'm impressed."

"What is it?" Jillian wanted to know.

"It's a Moose Crossing sign. You know, a yellow sign with a silhouette of a moose on it?"

"Another moose reference," Jillian said. "Take a pic."

"You can't see it now," I said. "but, I can still see the backside. I'll take a pic of that."

The corgis immediately calmed and settled back to their seat.

"What does a moose have to do with our missing penguin chick?" Shannon asked. She activated the van's signal and turned right, onto Kramer Ave. "I'm so fascinated by your dogs, Mr. Anderson. Er, Zack. Sorry."

"It's okay. Tell you what, if you ever figure out how Sherlock and Watson do it, be sure to let us know. I'm still trying to figure it all out."

"Is this the same way you brought us in last time?" Jillian suddenly asked. "This doesn't look familiar."

"You're very observant," Shannon said, as she briefly locked eyes with my wife in the rearview mirror. "We used a more direct route last time. This time around, I thought I'd show you more of the town itself. These houses, for example, most of them have redundant energy systems in place. See the solar panels? And how every house has multiple chimneys?"

"In case the weather causes them to lose power, is that it?" Jillian guessed.

"Exactly. You cannot survive out here if the power goes out. And if it does, it can sometimes stay that way for close to a week."

"Does that happen often?" I asked, amazed. "I would think that'd be dangerous."

"You'd be surprised just how much we look out for one another. If someone's house goes dark, then there will usually be three or four neighbors checking on them before the day's end."

"I like that," Jillian said. "We have that same mentality in Pomme Valley."

Shannon met our eyes in the mirror.

"Pomme Valley? Love the name of the town. And is that in Washington?"

"Oregon," I corrected. "It's a small town that's fairly close to a medium-sized one, which works out just fine for us."

We felt the van slow and saw that we had a sharp turn coming up.

"We're now approaching Harbor Mountain Road," Shannon reported.

"I remember that from yesterday," Jillian said. "CCCP is at the end of the road, isn't it? At the top?"

"Yes. You've got a good memory."

"Hey," I protested, holding up a hand, "I remember it was at the end of the road, too."

Jillian patted my hand.

"That's such a good boy."

Shannon snorted, as she smiled at me.

"I like you two. You're great together."

I took my wife's hand in my own.

"Yeah, she's a keeper."

Once we were back inside the main facility and our coats, scarves, mittens, earmuffs, and doggie coats were all hanging in the entry closet, we saw Dr. Marianne Rozhkov descend the stairs. She smiled at the two of us before holding out twin laminated cards.

"Take these. Clip them to your shirts. They'll get you access to everywhere in the complex. Should you decide entry into the penguin exhibits is needed, I just ask that you let us know first. That way, we can make sure we keep our birds out of the way."

I clipped the badge to my shirt and looked down at the dogs.

"Sherlock, Watson—are you two ready to go?"

I got head-tilts from both dogs.

"I take it that's a yes," Dr. Rozhkov said. "Please, if you find anything, or have any questions, don't hesitate to call me."

"And how do we do that?" Jillian asked.

Marianne pointed at a phone on a nearby table.

"From anywhere in the facility, press the asterisk twice. The phone at my desk will ring. If I'm not there to answer, then the system will automatically route it to my cell."

"Impressive," Jillian said.

"Evil," Dr. Rozhkov countered. "It's what happens when your IT guy happens to be quite good at telephony systems."

I snapped my fingers.

"Speaking of which, has he been able to get anything from that camera we found yesterday?"

Dr. Rozhkov blinked a few times. "That's right. I should have heard from him by now. I'll go find out myself, and then I'll let you know."

"Sounds good. Well, guys, you've been waiting for this." I leaned forward to unclip their leashes. "Have at it. Let's see if we can figure out what's going on around here, okay?"

I had no sooner dropped their leashes when Sherlock lifted his nose, sniffed once, and then turned to look at the door we had just come through.

"We're not leaving yet, pal. We've got work to do. So, now's the time to impress us. Do your magic. Where do you want to go?"

Apparently, the answer to that question was the main door. Sherlock and Watson trotted over to the door, sniffed along the base, and then sat.

"You can't possibly have to go potty," I told them. "It's the door leading outside. We just came through. What about it?"

Jillian approached the door and ran her fingers along the surface. While she did that, I decided I wanted a closer look.

"It's a door, guys. I'd say about seven feet tall. There aren't any windows, it's been stained a dark brown, and there's a single peephole, low enough for a leprechaun to look through without needing a ladder."

Overhearing, Marianne burst out laughing.

"The only thing we can figure is that the previous owners must have been disabled, and in a wheelchair."

I stared at the peephole, then the door in general, and finally, down at the dogs.

"A wheelchair, huh? Well, in that case, why's there a coat hanger way the heck up there, near the top of the door?"

Dr. Rozhkov shrugged. She didn't know.

Rising up on my tiptoes, I felt along the antique coat hooks and immediately stopped. There were two hooks, a top and a bottom. Both, with a little elbow grease, could be positioned to the left or right. However, there was something on the backside of the top hook that wasn't on the lower one. Stretching up as high as I could go, I managed to get a firm enough grip on the thing to pull it away.

A suction noise, like the ripping of duct tape, could be heard.

"What do you have there, Zachary?" Jillian asked.

I held the small, circular gray dot up and studied it.

"It looks like a bug. Dr. Rozhkov, you might want to have your IT guy check this out, too."

"What is it?" Marianne asked, overhearing. "Omigod, is that what I think it is?"

"You've been bugged," I confirmed. "It shouldn't

come as too much of a surprise, seeing how we've already found a camera."

Marianne took the tiny piece of surveillance equipment and glared at it. If I didn't know any better, I'd say she was going to step on it.

"Hey, let it go, okay? That's why we're here. And in case we find anything else, you might want to give us a bag, or a box."

"I certainly hope you don't," Marianne muttered. "I'll be right back."

"Why would someone go to so much trouble to bug a penguin breeding center?" Jillian asked, as she watched me fold up the plastic grocery bag and shove it in my pocket. "I don't understand why someone would care that much. Are they not doing something worthwhile? Is it not in everyone's best interests to let them succeed?"

"Since when has that stopped anyone from doing a dastardly deed?" I returned. "If there's a buck to be made, or an advantage to be had, then you'd better believe there's a lowlife out there who'll never question how low he has to stoop."

"That's disheartening," Jillian decided. "Where are we headed now?"

We had been following the corgis as they slowly sniffed around the seating area. The fireplace had once more been lit. A bin of firewood was nearby, and a set of fireplace tools, including a poker, shovel, and brush, were on the opposite side. Sherlock sniffed once and moved on.

"I'm not sure. What's through there? The

kitchen?"

I was right. The kitchen was next. Several of the keepers were there, prepping food for the penguins' diets. All three were women, and none of them looked to be over thirty. The closest, a pale woman with long blonde hair looked up as she weighed several fish on a scale. She gave us a quizzical look before she noticed the dogs. Both eyes then shot open and she promptly forgot about the fish still on the scale.

"This is them! Oh! I can't believe it! I recognize you from television!"

There was something about her accent. Definitely European. Maybe Scandinavian?

"Hello," I said, and started to hold out my hand. "Zack Anderson. This is my wife, Jillian, and something tells me you know Sherlock and Watson?"

"I'm so very pleased to meet you!" the blonde woman cried. "I'm Sigrid. Sigrid Magnussen. You can call me Siggie. They all do."

"Hi, Siggie," Jillian said, waving. "I'd shake your hand but, um ..."

"*Ja*, my hands. Disgusting. We meet later, eh? Would love to take some pictures!"

I looked at the next woman over, who was neither smiling nor frowning. She had a stern look about her features, was tall, almost as tall as me, and had high, prominent cheekbones. Her brown hair had been braided and was worn down her back. She studied me with cold, intelligent eyes, but once she saw the corgis, her features softened.

"You right, Siggie," she said, with a heavy Russian accent. "Adorable, like pictures. Katia Petrov. Call me Katia."

I nodded, and noticed Katia was up to her elbows in fish guts, too.

"Katia it is. Hello! It's good to meet you."

We turned to the third keeper. This one, wisely enough, was wearing rubber gloves, like those you'd wear to protect your hands while washing dishes, and was carefully inserting large white pills into the fish, through the gills. She was shorter than Jillian, at about five-feet-two, and had jet black hair. I would even go so far as to say her hair was dyed, since it looked like her roots were red. She had several visible tattoos on her right arm, and her left had a sleeve of various images, all jumbled together. I also noticed several nose rings, one piercing through her right eyebrow, and at least five or six piercings in each ear.

"Hi!" the woman holding the pills said. There were no accents detectable. "I'm Penny Rees. You're from Oregon, aren't you? And your dogs? You met the Queen of England, didn't you?"

"We did," I confirmed. "It's nice to meet you, Penny. So, where are you three from? How long have you been here?"

"Stockholm," Siggie cheerfully supplied, without looking up from her work station. "I've known Dr. Rozhkov for about six months now."

"Vladivostok," Katia announced. She tapped her

chest. "Russian. Two weeks have I been here."

"Russia, huh?" I said, trying to be polite and keep the conversation going. "I've always wanted to see it."

Katia's nose lifted. "Hmmph."

Okay. I won't be making friends with that one. For what reason would she not like me? Maybe ... maybe she was worried that I might find out she had her hand in all the problems CCCP has been having? Perhaps she knew something about the hidden spy equipment we've found? Could she be some type of KGB agent?

I dismissed the idea almost as quickly as it had come to me. For crying out loud, the KGB didn't even exist anymore. See? This is what happens when writers start thinking too much.

"I'm from Iowa," Penny reported. "Born and raised. I've only been here two weeks, too."

"Iowa," I repeated, smiling. "Sounds like you loved it."

"You couldn't be more wrong," Penny replied, as she grabbed another fish and inserted a pill. "The moment I was old enough, I lit out of there like I was a cat in a dog show."

Jillian held up a hand. "Penny, can I ask what you're doing?"

"Sure. My parents were so strict that ... oh. You're asking about this? I'm inserting vitamin supplements into some of the fish. It's the easiest way to get a penguin to take their vitamins, let me tell you. Insert through the gills here and then presto, right down the hatch."

I felt a tap on my shoulder. Turning, I saw Jillian pointing at the dogs. This time, the two of them were staring at the large walk-in freezer.

"We're not going in there," I told the dogs. "I don't care how much you whine. Nuh-uh. Not happening."

I heard Penny laugh. Looking up, I caught Katia in the midst of a smile, but she quickly sobered once she saw me watching. Siggie was humming to herself, oblivious to the conversation, and busy with her work.

I handed the leashes to Jillian and approached the freezer.

"*Awwoooooo*," Sherlock howled, but it was so low, it was almost a growl.

"There must be something wrong with the freezer," Jillian said. "Maybe they're looking at the door? Let me try this. Sherlock, Watson, come here. We're going to walk by the freezer, Zachary. See if they do anything, okay?"

I watched my wife parade the dogs past the freezer. I saw both dogs look at the handle, but that was about it.

"Still looks like they want to go inside," I decided.

"*Nyet*, they don't," Katia stated. "You watched them just like me, *da*?"

"*Da*. Er, yes. Why?"

"They looked there, near handle."

"Near handle," I repeated. "Let's see. The dial? It's

just a temperature gauge. It shows how …" I trailed off as I looked at Katia, who was returning my stare as though I had sprouted another head. I turned to the dogs. "It tells the temperature, that's all."

"*Идиот*. Idiot. If that is temperature gauge, then what is that?"

I followed Katia's finger and gasped. There, above the door was a digital readout, which also gave me the freezer's temperature. However, it did *not* match the gauge by the handle.

"How long has this been here?" Jillian wanted to know.

Three sets of shoulders shrugged.

"It's been here as long as I have," Siggie answered, overhearing the question.

I pointed at the counter. "Could I borrow that knife there?"

"You'd better get it, *Sötis*," Siggie said, batting her eyes. "I be smellin' like a fish at the moment."

"*Sötis*?" I quietly asked, as I turned to my wife.

"She says *cutie*," came a quiet voice.

Turning, we were surprised to see Katia standing so close, we were practically touching shoulders.

"She likes you. Here, I wash hands. This is knife. What will you do?"

I took the knife and carefully inserted the tip beneath the oval analog gauge. I gave the knife a quick flick, and the entire circular instrument popped off. The remnants of a piece of two-sided tape were visible. Turning the device over, I saw that the back cover could come off. Using the knife a second time, I removed the cover and let out a breath: a tiny camera was concealed inside.

"Jillian, remind me to pick up some doggie biscuits at the first opportunity we can, okay?"

"Of course, Zachary. Katia, thank you."

The Russian keeper held out a hand. Shrugging, I passed the camera to her.

"Clever. It makes me … mad. Someone is watching? Right now?"

"I don't think it has the ability to stream a live image," I said. "It probably records what it sees and then uploads it somewhere on the Internet."

Katia held the disguised camera out to me.

"Dr. Rozhkov will want to see this, *da*?"

"Definitely. Thanks. I'll get it to her."

Nodding, Katia rejoined her fellow keepers and returned to work.

The corgis, satisfied that they had discovered all they needed to here in the kitchen, moved off.

"I don't get it," I said, an hour later. I held my grocery bag up and looked at the six cameras and ten listening devices we had found since we started our investigation, and that was only on the ground floor. "What's the big deal? Why is someone so adamant about watching and listening to what goes on inside this place? Correct me if I'm wrong, but is this, or is this not, just a place to breed penguins? Why is there so much interest?"

"I can understand the incubation room," Jillian

said, as we paused at the base of the staircase and looked up. "After all, we found two bugs in that one room, and two cameras. One was pointed at the incubator, and the other on the work table. The rest of these? I'm as lost as you are."

"*Woof.*"

It had become routine. I looked at Sherlock, saw where he was looking, and went for whatever was in his line of sight. This time, it was a small, plush animal up on a shelf across from the staircase. However, the offending item was just a little too far out of my reach. Thankfully, I remembered seeing a broom in the entry closet after I had hung our outer wear to dry upon our arrival.

Once I had knocked the stuffed animal off its perch, and caught it before it could fall to the floor, I handed it to Jillian while the broom was returned. By the time I made it back, my wife had extricated a tiny pin camera and its battery pack from within the stuffed walrus.

"They certainly are persistent," she observed, as I held open my bag, like a trick-or-treater, and watched the small camera join the others.

"Any luck?" Dr. Rozhkov asked, moments later.

I held out the bag and watched Marianne's face turn a bright shade of red.

"You're kidding. Are you effin' kidding me?"

I stifled a chuckle while Jillian had to look away.

"I'm so sorry. I shouldn't swear."

"You didn't," I pointed out. "*Effin'* doesn't really count, but it does get the point across."

"Have you finished searching?" Marianne wanted to know.

"Only the ground floor, I'm afraid."

"My god. You haven't even been to the second floor yet? Or to the infirmary?"

"No, ma'am," I confirmed.

Dr. Rozhkov looked inside the bag a second time and, if possible, grew angrier. She pulled out her phone and dialed a number.

"Chris. I need you to drop what you're doing and come in. Now. No, the database can wait. I'm holding a bag full of electronic surveillance equipment that someone placed inside CCCP. I need you to work your magic and tell me how long they've been here and, more importantly, who's responsible. Yes, I'll authorize the overtime, just get in here now. Thank you."

"Your IT guy?" I guessed.

"Yes. He's young, but he's absolutely brilliant. Don't ever tell him I said that."

Two hours later, we were done with our inspection of the entire facility. I'm sorry to say that an additional eight cameras and fifteen audio bugs were recovered, much to Dr. Rozhkov's dismay. But, I will say that Chris Emery, a young kid of nineteen, had finally arrived and set up his temporary station in CCCP's control room. He was slightly on the heavy side, wore faded blue jeans, and a Captain America t-shirt. His thick, curly hair needed to be brushed, and he had two or three days' worth of growth on his face. He looked up as we walked in, which resulted in his wire-rimmed glasses sliding down his nose. The teenager angrily pushed them back up as I watched his eyes travel down the leashes until they were resting on the dogs.

"Them? They're the ones who found all this stuff? Oh, sorry. I'm Chris."

I shook the kid's hand.

"Zack Anderson. This is my wife, Jillian. Down there, staring up at you, is Sherlock and Watson. Sherlock has black in his fur, and Watson has just the red and white in hers, no black."

"Hers? Watson is a girl?"

I laughed.

"Long story. Here, might as well add these to your collection."

"Holy crap! All this, too?"

"Yes. Someone really wanted to keep tabs on this place. Any idea who?"

Chris shrugged.

"I have no idea. We're up in the middle of nowhere. You can't drive a car to get here, so we're fairly isolated. I don't think I've ever heard Dr. Rozhkov raise her voice except for today."

"She was shouting at someone?" I asked, eager for some news. I pulled out my notebook. "Do you know who?"

"Of course, I do. Me! I can tell you, it wasn't fun."

Jillian's eyes softened. "I'm sure she's not mad at you. I think she's just frustrated."

Chris hefted the bag of electronics.

"Yeah, I guess I can see why that would be."

"Will you be able to trace where those things are sending their data?" I asked.

"I should. It's just a matter of plugging it into my computer, determining what its MAC addy is, and then accessing the log files. Now, if I open my ASCII editor here, and tell it to display that file there, then ... yes, look! I have an IP address, and I can tell you it's a local one."

"A local *what*?" I asked. "Business? Computer? Evil mastermind?"

"Huh? What? No, I'm still talking about the IP address. Let me scrub it against known gateways and ... there we go! It's from GCI, a local high-speed cable internet service. That means that this camera sends the footage it records to someone in town. What they do with it after that, I can't say."

"What about the others?" I asked, pointing at the bag of goodies he was still holding.

"I'll start going through them. It all depends on whether or not I can connect to them and get my computer to recognize the device. I don't know about the audio bugs, but the cameras should reveal the results."

"We're going to keep talking to the staff here," I said, gathering up the dogs' leashes. "If you find anything, would you let us know?"

"You got it."

"Who do you want to talk to, Zachary?" Jillian asked as we left the room, heading toward the front sitting room. Doors were everywhere. I figured there had to be somewhere else to look out there. "We've already talked to Marianne, and her assistant, Shannon. Then there's the three keepers from the kitchen. Finally, we just met Chris, the IT guy. Who else is there?"

"Is that really everyone?" I asked. "I just assumed there were more people here. Okay, what about the medical floor beneath us? We haven't spoken with whoever runs the show down there."

"Do we even know whose area it is?" my wife asked.

"That'd be mine," a new voice piped up.

"*Woof.*"

"*Rrrrrr.*"

"She growled again," I observed, amazed. "Watson never growls at …"

I trailed off as Watson finally looked up at the intruder and wriggled with delight. My timid little girl had lost her nervousness and was now hurrying to the stranger's side. The thin, young black man smiled, displaying a mouth full of bright, white teeth. Dressed in a white doctor's coat, a blue buttoned-down business shirt, and black slacks, he saw the approaching corgis and immediately lowered himself to the ground.

"These must be the two dogs I've heard so much about. Sherlock and Watson? Are those your names?"

"*Oooooooo,*" Watson agreed.

"So very nice to meet you both. And you two? You're their handlers? I'm sorry, their parents?"

"Zack Anderson, and this is my wife, Jillian. You're the one in charge of the infirmary?"

"Dr. Malek Tanko, at your service. Yes, I oversee Wellness."

"Wellness?" I repeated. "Your floor has a name?"

Dr. Tanko shrugged. "Wellness. Or infirmary. Either will do. Is it true? You found listening devices in my department?"

"We found bugs and cameras in all departments," Jillian corrected.

"They must have been placed here before the facility opened," Dr. Tanko theorized.

"Do you think it's possible?" I asked.

"I have been with Dr. Rozhkov from the beginning," the kindly veterinarian informed us. "It was very well known that this house would be turned into a research facility. Prior to CCCP's arrival, it sat, abandoned."

"For how long?" Jillian wanted to know.

"Two years, I believe."

"That means anyone could have hidden those devices," I groaned.

"Not all of them, Zachary," my wife argued. "Yes, some could have been well hidden, in places not affected by renovation. Others, though, would have to be placed. Individually. Dr. Tanko, if I were to ask you who you think could be responsible for this theft, would you have an answer for me?"

"Several. I assume you need to interrogate them?"

"I was actually looking for people we might've

missed," I admitted. "There's Dr. Rozhkov and her assistant, the three animal keepers who are all from different countries, you, and Chris, the tech guy. Did we leave anyone out?"

"There are four keepers," Dr. Tanko corrected. "I saw Sigrid earlier, and Katia. I also saw the American, Penny. Those are the three you've met?"

Both Jillian and I nodded.

"That means you still haven't met Isabeau. Isabeau Fontaine. She's French. She ..."

The Nigerian doctor trailed off as the front door opened and admitted someone wearing a bright blue snow suit, a thick wool hat, and ski goggles. She set her duffel on the floor and began peeling off layers.

"*Je n'y crois pas*. It's too soon for snow! I just had to get a job in Alaska. Oh! Visitors! How wonderful!"

"She's from France?" I quietly asked the doctor. "I don't hear an accent at all, not even when she's speaking in French."

"She speaks perfect English," Dr. Tanko contradicted, "and I thought her accent was quite distinguishable."

I looked at Jillian, who held out her hands, indicating she couldn't hear an accent either.

"I love your dogs. They will love me, *n'est-ce pas*? Bonjour, you lovely boys!"

Isabeau Fontaine's age matched the other keepers, in that she was probably in her mid-twenties. She had shoulder-length straight brown hair that somehow looked both tousled and natural-looking at the same time. Her skin was smooth and clear, and her face had a healthy-looking glow. Even though she was wearing a comfortable pair of jeans, paired with a soft white shirt and a black jacket, her outfit looked as though it had just come out of a fashion magazine.

"Just so you know," I began, "Watson is a girl."

"*C'est terrible!* Watson is no name for such a beautiful girl. You are evil man, are you not?"

Jillian snorted with laughter.

"You know I am teasing you, do you not? I am Isabeau. This is Watson? *Mon Dieu!* This is Sherlock, oui? I know these two! Their exploits-- *Très célèbre!*"

"Très *what*?" I caught the *very* part."

"Famous," Jillian translated.

I looked at my wife and smiled. It shouldn't surprise me, after all, she can read the menu at her beloved Chateau restaurant and it was all in French.

"Er, how long have you worked here?" I asked. My notebook found its way into my hands.

"Two months. Already! Two wonderful months. I love it here, but the weather? Gives me *un mal de tête*."

Exasperated, I turned to Jillian.

"Headache," my wife translated again.

Isabeau nodded. "*Mais oui*. But, I learn to live with it. For the penguins, I adapt. *Excusez-moi*, I must be off."

"There's no way it could be her," I said, as soon as the French woman had disappeared through the doorway leading to the kitchen.

"I'm inclined to agree," Jillian said. "Although, it could be an act."

"Then, it's a very good act. But, did you notice the dogs?"

"They both loved her."

"That's right, they did. It also means that we've met everyone here. Sherlock and Watson didn't zero in on any of them. Do you know what that means?"

"It's not an inside job," Jillian guessed.

"Exactly. No one else has access. Who could it be? My dear, I've got to tell you that I'm starting to think the chick never left the premises. Granted, we'd need to let Sherlock and Watson do a thorough check of the exhibits to rule it out."

"I don't think we'll be allowed," Jillian reported. "I remember what Dr. Hawk said to us when we were in Monterey. Outside animals are never allowed to encounter those that are on the inside. They can't risk contamination. Besides, those yards have been thoroughly examined by the staff. If the chick was out there, or worse, if it was out there and no longer alive, they would've found it. No, I don't think it'll be necessary to get the dogs in the penguin yards. The chick isn't here."

Chris emerged from the doorway leading to the control room and beckoned us to follow him.

"I've tracked two others. Cameras, I mean.

They're in town. Everything I've managed to trace all leads to town."

"Are they the same IP?" I asked.

"Yes. I've checked it twice. They're the same address. That means that someone in town is getting daily updates on what we've been doing. I've since switched to a stronger encryption code, remotely logged off everyone listed in the DHCP tables, and am now requiring password changes for everyone. What are they doing?"

I looked down at the dogs. Sherlock and Watson were staring at the large video display at the main control console. Instead of looking at a number of video feeds, like it typically displayed, we were now looking at a computer desktop. Chris must have been sitting at the computer to do his tracing. The dogs, however, wouldn't budge.

"Oh, come on, guys. Really?"

Jillian sighed and shook her head. "Just do it, Zachary. Why do you act surprised?"

"But ... but ... fine. Whatever. Here, guys. I'm taking a picture of the computer. There, I took two. Happy?"

Satisfied, Sherlock and Watson rose to their feet, gave themselves a good shake, and headed to the closest door. I looked at Chris.

"I guess that means we're done for the day."

FOUR

T he third day of our impromptu Alaskan trip found us exploring downtown Sitka. With a population of over eight thousand people, the town was considered small, but it was still nearly three times the size of Pomme Valley. The five of us, including Shannon, our guide, perused the shops lining Lincoln Street as we slowly passed by.

Personally, I didn't think I'd be seeing this particular town again. After all, Jillian and I were here last year, for our first ever cruise together. We hadn't really explored the city. Rather, after disembarking at the pier, all we really did was check out the shops catering to the tourists who lingered in the area, waiting for their excursions to begin. As for us, we booked a whale-watching trip on a smaller boat with a local guide, who absolutely guaranteed we'd find whales or else we'd get our money back. It was a boisterous claim, and one I was eager to collect on, since let's face it, my luck stinks. However, we hit gold. Not only did we see a pod of humpback whales, but also a large raft of otters, multiple bald eagle nests, and quite a few seals. That particular trip ended with a fantastic crab dinner at the Fin Island Lodge. If you ever go, it's well worth the price.

This time, Jillian and I were walking, hand-in-hand, outside. The corgis were once more in their jackets. Jillian was in full Eskimo mode, with a heavy coat, fur-lined hood, scarf, earmuffs, and mittens. I had on my black Disneyland sweatshirt, with a large, irritable dwarf on the back, a regular tee shirt, and jeans. Oh, let me tell you, I got the looks. Everyone I passed was dressed to the hilt. Me? You'd think it was summertime and I was out, taking my dogs for a walk.

It was a balmy forty degrees outside. It was not cool enough to snow, but not really warm enough to melt the snowfall from yesterday. Then again, the sidewalks had been shoveled and salted. Looking at the rock salt scattered across the cement got me thinking: was it safe for dogs to walk on it?

The Fates intervened and presented an answer. We were approaching a pet store. Jillian and Shannon, who were in the middle of a discussion about small towns and their attractive qualities, stopped once they saw me point at the door.

"Let's head inside. I want to see if they have booties for the dogs."

Jillian stifled a giggle. "You've tried getting them booties before. It didn't go over well. Are you sure you want to try again?"

I pointed at the salt beneath our feet.

"I don't know if that's gonna bother the dogs. I'd prefer not to worry about it, so yes, I'd like to try again to get them fitted with shoes."

"*This* I have to see," Shannon said, giving us a smile.

Once we were indoors, and I told the friendly proprietor what we were looking for, we were taken to a sitting area where we, the humans, were told to wait, like the dogs. Seriously, my lips quivered as soon as she told us to sit. Shannon snorted with laughter.

However, ten minutes later *I* was the one laughing. Sherlock and Watson were fitted with zipper boots made of neoprene. Each of the boots had soles that could help with traction on ice-covered ground. The laughter came when the dogs tried walking.

I urge you to look up the following term: goose-stepping. Have you seen archival footage of armies all marching in step, only their steps were taken by lifting their legs—without bending the knees—several feet off the ground? The Nazis were probably the most well-known users of this marching style.

Well, that's what my little dogs looked like. Not caring for the boots one bit, both corgis lifted their stumpy little legs as high as they could, no doubt thinking they would be able to step out of the footwear. No such luck, I'm afraid.

I couldn't look at them without laughing. Jillian tried, quite valiantly I might add, but she ended up giggling, too. The last time we tried to get the dogs to wear boots, I received such a severe case of stink-eye that I ended up apologizing. This time around, both dogs acted as though they knew we were trying to help them. I kept getting side glances from Sherlock, but surprisingly enough, that's all he did.

"If there's a corgi hell," I began, as we pushed the door open to head back out, "then I just bought myself a condo. That is, hands down, one of the funniest things I've ever seen."

"They're taking to them quite well," Shannon observed. "Yes, they may not care for them, but it looks like they're trying."

"What would you say Sitka's main industry is?" Jillian asked, after we moved off from admiring some jewelry in a display.

"That's easy," Shannon answered. "Tourism. After all, look at these stores. How many jewelry stores does one town need?"

I paused to look back at the street. She was right. Every third store advertised a sale on diamonds, or tanzanite, or some other type of precious stone.

A few moments later, the answer came to me.

"Cruises. They're catering to people taking cruises."

Shannon nodded. "Exactly. Can you imagine what would happen if those giant ships stop docking at our ports? The money would dry up in no time."

"There's gotta be something to fall back on beside tourism?" I protested. "Mining? Er, lumber?"

"There's fishing," Shannon said. "But, as you can imagine, come wintertime, many of the freshwater inlets will freeze solid. Those that don't will have so many large chunks of ice floating around in the water that fishermen won't risk heading out. Their whole lives are dependent on their summer catches."

"Did this used to be a mining town?" I asked, curious.

"Gold mining and fish canning were what started Sitka's initial growth," Shannon reported.

My brow wrinkled. "Fish canning? That sounds positively disgusting."

Shannon nodded. "For us? Now? Absolutely. For those without refrigeration? Those looking to safely store enough supplies to make it through the harsh winters? It was very popular."

"And you said there was gold mining? Any idea how much was discovered?" I asked.

Our guide shrugged. "If you're willing to put in the hard work, and understand that there are processes the gold must go through in order to be usable, then sure."

"You can say *no*, you know," I told her, grinning. "Sounds like mining done by individuals wouldn't be worth it, but a huge corporation with the funds to acquire all the necessary equipment? I'm sure they could be able to turn a decent profit."

"When was the area first settled?" Jillian asked.

We had just approached a clothing store and my wife naturally paused.

"Oh, gosh, do you know what? I really don't know, I'm sorry."

I pulled out my phone. "I'm on it. Let's see. Wow. I wouldn't have called it. The answer is 1799, founded by one Alexander Baranov, who just so happened to be the governor of Russian America. Huh. You learn something new every day."

"If you really want to know what keeps the money flowing in Sitka," Shannon began, "it'd be fishing. Look."

We had reached a cross street, allowing us to look southwest. There, just a short walk away, was Crescent Harbor. Fleets of small fishing boats, with a few larger ones mixed in, were bobbing in the waves. As I stared at the boats, I was reminded of something I had heard Shannon say: CCCP purchased the surrounding land. Could they have acquired the property under shady circumstances?

"Penny for your thoughts," Jillian softly told me.

"I was thinking about the ten acres CCCP owns."

"What about it?" Shannon wanted to know.

"You told us that Dr. Rozhkov was able to convince the city to sell her the ten acres."

"Yes, that's right."

"Who owned it before?" I wanted to know.

"Originally? Private owners, but at the time, the land belonged to the city."

"Meaning we could have a highly-irritated former land owner out there holding a grudge?"

Jillian stopped to look at me, and then gave Shannon a questioning look.

"Is that possible? Could we have a disgruntled land owner angry at CCCP?"

Shannon was on her phone, typing furiously away. "I'm not sure. I can check with Dr. Rozhkov."

"I think the land may be key," I said. "Find out what you can. Who owned it, whether or not someone lived on it, or was planning to. Prior to the purchase, what was it being used for? That sort of thing."

Shannon nodded and continued to tap away on her phone's display.

We continued on our walking tour when the dogs came to an abrupt stop. This time, we were at a small mom-and-pop drug store. Jillian and I stared at each other for a few moments before staring at the sign: Lotus Blossom Apothecary.

"Why did the dogs stop here?" Jillian wanted to know.

I shrugged. "Maybe they caught a whiff of something they couldn't identify? It doesn't really matter, since they aren't sitting. Let's … well, I was just proven wrong. Come on, guys. That was much too long of a delay. Can we get going, please?"

Neither dog budged.

My hands were full of leashes, and the dogs had managed to twist in place a few times, effectively tangling them together. There was no way I was going to make it to my phone. Thankfully, Jillian came to my rescue by retrieving my cell from my pocket, taking a quick picture of the store, and then slipping it back in. Satisfied, the dogs rose to their feet and trotted on, without a care in the world.

Or goose-stepped, I suppose. I still thought it was funny. A sobering thought occurred, one that wiped the smirk from my face. Was this payback from Sherlock? Would he deliberately fake a corgi clue just to get back at me?

Sighing, I gave the dogs a pat on the head, which went largely unnoticed. I couldn't take the chance of ignoring their actions, and I'm sure those little boogers knew it. Shannon suddenly pointed across the street.

"There it is. The local office for GCI. Do you really think you can persuade them to give us the information from what Chris found?"

I untangled the leashes and pointed at the sign with three large, red letters.

"Let's go find out. Come on."

Once we were all inside the small office, which consisted of nothing more than a large desk, a bookcase on one wall, and a set of folding tables on the other, we took a look around. On the tables were an assortment of equipment: modems, power supplies, network cables, and coax cables. An older woman, with bright orange hair and a pair of glasses perched precariously on the tip of her nose, looked up from her desk. She immediately smiled and waved us over.

"Come in, come in! It's awfully chilly out there, isn't? Heavens, I thought I knew everyone in town, but I don't recognize any of you."

Shannon held up a hand. "I've been in town a few months now. These two haven't."

"We're just visiting," I announced. After a few moments, I held out a hand. "I'm Zack Anderson. This is my wife, Jillian. Down there are Sherlock and Watson."

"They're corgis, aren't they? My goodness, I wish I had something to give you pretty boys."

Watson snorted once, as though she knew she had just been identified incorrectly, but settled down almost immediately. When no goodies were forthcoming, both dogs sank into a down position next to my feet.

"Virginia Poulson. Call me Ginny. How can I help you today?"

I was ready to ask her about the IP address when Marianne's warning sounded in my mind. She didn't want to alert anyone to the theft of their penguin chick. How, then, could I get the information we needed without arousing any suspicion?

"I'm looking for my niece," I began, which instantly had both of my female companions turning to look at me. "I received an email from her a while back, and I was relieved to hear she was okay. However, her messages stopped quite abruptly, and it has my family concerned. I know she's somewhere in town, but I just don't know where. Her email address ended with *gci.com*, so I know she's a customer here. Is there anything you can do to help me out?"

"What's her email address?" Ginny asked.

"I'm sorry, I don't have that," I confessed. "And before you say anything, yes, I should have written it down."

"You came all the way out here without at least one of her messages printed out?" Ginny suspiciously asked. "How did you think you were going to track her down?"

I held up the piece of paper Chris had handed me the day before.

"Well, I have an IP address, if it helps."

Ten minutes later, we had an actual physical address.

"I can't tell you how impressed I am," Jillian told me, once we had left the internet provider's office and were headed back to the van. "How'd you come up with a story like that so fast?"

"I just asked myself what type of story I'd have to hear in order to get me to be willing to help. It's the first thing that came to mind."

"Shannon, do you know where we can find Merrill Street?" Jillian asked.

Our guide took the slip of paper and studied the address. "No, but I'm sure my phone can find it. Let's see. Merrill ... here it is. It's north of us. According to this, it's less than five minutes from here."

"Walking?' I asked, surprised.

"No, driving."

Turns out, we weren't as lucky as I had hoped. The address turned out to be a small rental condo, and it had been cleared out. Very recently, from what we could tell by looking through the windows. There were a few empty boxes stacked along the wall. A threadbare couch was visible in the front room. Coat hangers had been scattered across the floor, as if someone had rapidly yanked their clothing off their holders.

"Now what?" I wanted to know. "Our one lead just hit a dead-end."

Shannon perked up. "I have an idea. It may be a long shot, but I think since this is such a small town, we may have a chance."

"What's your idea?" Jillian asked.

Shannon pointed south, toward town.

"You've seen the size of Sitka. There are only a few bars here. I say we go down there and start with the most popular one, and work our way down the list if need be. Everyone around here loves their favorite bars. It's the ultimate place to hang out and socialize."

"I'm assuming we're still trying to keep CCCP's name out of this, right?" I added.

Shannon nodded. "Right."

The first place we found was Burt's Old Time Saloon. It wasn't hard to miss, seeing how we walked by it earlier in the day. We were back on Lincoln Street, and as we approached the hanging wooden sign, we all heard loud, raucous laughter coming from within.

"I think I'll stay out here," Jillian said, as she took the leashes from me. "You and Shannon go on in."

Nodding, I gave my wife a quick peck on her cheek and held the door open for Shannon, who oddly enough, blushed bright red before hurrying inside.

Burt's Old Time Saloon was the epitome of a dive bar. Two pool tables were to the left, as you came inside. Four booths were opposite from the pool tables. Directly ahead were a number of wood hexagonal tables, each with four rickety chairs scattered around it. Against the far wall, straight ahead, was the counter. A young, bearded fellow was there, drying a set of beer mugs and watching us intently.

"Afternoon," the bartender said, pleasantly enough. "Can I get you two something? Beer? Glass of wine?"

"Do you make your own here?" I asked.

"Afraid not. I'd love to someday. You're not from around here, are you?"

Shannon raised a hand. "I am, he isn't."

"Where're you from, buddy?" I was asked.

"Oregon. Probably a little place you've never heard of before. Pomme Valley?"

The bartender's eyes widened. "What are the odds of that happening? I *have* heard about a little town in Oregon. Something to do with a couple of those low-rider dogs the Queen of England loved.

In fact, I see two of them just outside. Wait. Wait just a damn minute. If you're gonna tell me those two are who I *think* they are, well, you just got yourself a free beer on the house."

"Sherlock and Watson?" I ventured, giving my new friend a smile.

"Holy crap! I've seen those dogs on TV!"

"With the Queen? Yep, that's them."

"Yo, Sheila! Get out here! You ain't gonna believe this!"

An Inuit woman about the same age as Shannon appeared, wiping her hands on a towel.

"Whatcha need, Matt?"

A finger was pointed my way.

"What's the name of those two dogs you were telling me about last week? The ones who found some missing jewels and were on TV, meeting the queen?"

"Those corgis? Sherlock and Watson, why?"

Matt's finger swiveled until he was pointing outside.

"That's them, right there."

"Get out of here. That's not them."

"They really are," I offered. I held a hand out to the lady. "Zack Anderson. My wife, Jillian, is outside, holding the leashes."

"Get outta town," Sheila scoffed. "There's no way you can convince me that …"

At this point, Matt thrust his phone in Sheila's hands. On the display was a familiar sight. Well, it was familiar to me. Jillian and I were exchanging vows, in Westminster Abbey. There, clearly visible, was the late Queen of England.

Sheila's eyes widened as they stared at the screen, then up at me, then back at the phone's display.

"It's you! It's really you! You … you're famous! What're you doing here, in Alaska? A-*ha*! You're workin' a case!"

Oh, crap on a cracker. *Stick with the phony story, Zack*, I ordered myself.

"Actually, I was looking for a friend of mine," I began. "He was renting a place up on Merrill. It was a condo, I believe. However, I lost contact with him and thought I'd head up here. You know, to do a wellness check."

Shannon tapped my arm. She leaned forward, intent on passing some information to me in a confidential manner. Intrigued, I lowered my head.

"And if the person you're looking for happens to be a woman?" Shannon quietly asked.

Hmm, good point.

"Got a picture of your friend?" the bartender asked. "I don't think I've ever been asked to pick out someone based on where they live before."

"I understand," I said, thinking fast. "I was hoping that he'd stand out in a small town like this."

"Do you know for certain he came here?" the barkeep asked.

I shrugged. "This place is popular and Sitka is

small. I'd like to think he would have stopped by a few times."

"What's the timeframe involved?"

I looked at Shannon. "What, no more than two months?"

Shannon nodded. "Sounds right."

Matt stroked his beard and looked thoughtful. "Well, you're right. We don't get many outside people here, aside from tourist season. So, in order to be noticed by us, this person would have had to come in here more than once, or else do something to attract our attention. You follow?"

I sighed. "I see where you're going with this. That's okay. I'll keep looking for him."

"Two months," Matt repeated, thinking. He looked at Shannon. "Well, now that I think about it, I do remember *you* coming in here a few times."

Shannon nodded. "You've got a great selection of local beers."

Sheila wandered by again and overheard the comment.

"We've got the best selection in town. Mr. Anderson, you've got to try Tatooine."

Me being the Stars Wars fan that I am, had to comment.

"You guys have a beer named after Tatooine?"

"Tatooine Sunrise. Has a pinch of citrus and a little pine."

"It's not bitter, is it?" I asked. "I'm not a fan of bitter beers."

Matt set a small glass in front of me that had

several ounces of a light, golden beer. It was almost the same color as a pale orange juice.

"Well?" Matt prompted. Sheila was nearby, listening intently.

"It's actually quite good," I decided, smacking my lips. "Could I have a second glass? I want my wife to give it a try. Oh, Shannon? Have you tried this?"

"I have," Shannon confirmed. "I really like it, too."

Jillian came inside, and she enjoyed it more than I did, which isn't too surprising. She always told me her taste buds were more refined than this bottom feeder.

"We have a hit," I said, as I returned to the bar and handed the empty glass over. "Do you ship your beer?"

Matt nodded eagerly. "We do. What would you like?"

"Let's go with two cases of the Tatooine, thanks."

"We have about five other beers on tap," Sheila reminded me.

"With Star Wars names?" I asked, eager to add to my extensive collection of various sci-fi memorabilia.

"Oh, er, no."

"This will do for now, thanks."

While my order was being processed, and after I gave them a credit card to use, I heard the door open behind me. Thinking it might be Jillian, either changing her mind or wanting to change the order, I turned to look. A group of four locals entered, each around the same age as me, and claimed a table. Three of them were wearing rubber rain bibs, and the fourth wore a long-sleeved blue flannel shirt tucked into a pair of worn jeans. Sheila hurried over and took their orders.

"They got no business tellin' us what we can and can't do," one of the men grumbled. "I don't care if they are subsidizin' us. I've been makin' my livin' on the sea for all my life. I got no plans on stoppin' now."

"How long is the ban?" the guy wearing jeans asked.

"Through spring of next year."

Curses were bandied about.

Now, ordinarily, I would have tuned out this particular conversation. However, what they said next stopped me in my tracks.

"I'm just so damn tired of hearing how more and more areas are now off limits. How much is too much? At this rate, we won't be allowed to set our traps anywhere. It's a damn conspiracy, I tell you. What are you lookin' at, fella?"

"I'm sorry, I don't mean to pry, but did you just say the waters you're fishing are getting more and more restrictive?"

"Crabbing," I was sternly corrected.

"Sorry. Did you say they canceled the season? Why would they do that?"

"We had a decent season this summer," Mr. Blue Jeans told me. "Because it's just so-so, many of us, myself included, are forced to work outside our normal three month season. We ain't got no choice, you got me? And because of that, some fancy pants smartass thinks an extended season will hurt the population."

"I've seen the television shows," I protested. "That was something I never realized. Female lobsters are identified, marked, and tossed back. Is it the same for crabs?"

Blue Jeans nodded. "Gotta keep the population up. Harvestin' females are frowned upon. Word is, they're gonna make it illegal 'round here. Not yet, though. What do they think we are, idiots? Just because some jabbering dillhole thinks the population is low and needs time to rebound? What a load of crap! I seen what it looks like out there ..."

"... see," I whispered, knowing full well my wife would say the same thing if she had witnessed that grammatical atrocity.

"... and we are in no way worried about runnin' out of crab. Snow crab numbers are higher than they've ever been."

"How often do you guys lose access to certain patches of water?" I asked, hoping to steer the conversation to a more pleasant topic.

"Happens more'n ya think, pal," one of the other men said.

I cleared my throat. "Like if a certain

JEFFREY POOLE

organization opens up a facility and …"

"I was just beginnin' to like you, friend," Blue Jeans muttered, growing angry. "Don't tell me you're from that damn penguin place."

Sensing a growing hostility in the fishermen, I raised both hands and plastered my most harmless smile on my face. "Hey, no worries, guys. I'm not. I'm just a tourist here. Look, I'm buying a couple of cases of Alaskan beer for me and my friends back home."

The dark, accusatory looks vanished.

"Thanks for supportin' Burt's," Blue Jeans said, after a few moments had passed. He promptly turned to his companions and began complaining about something else.

I took the receipt for my beer and hurried Shannon out the door.

"Is everything okay?" my wife asked, once we made it outside.

"I think we have a new line of inquiry to check out," I said. I inclined my head at the bar. "You saw those fishermen who went in after me?"

"Yes."

"Something we didn't consider was how CCCP's arrival could affect the local fishing industry."

Jillian's eyes widened. "I hadn't thought of that. Excellent work, Zachary!"

"The water is a lot of people's life-blood," Shannon explained. "They make their living out there. I can also tell you that Dr. Rozhkov negotiated with the city to acquire some water

90

rights. I can't believe I didn't think about that until now."

"The fishing industry," I repeated, nodding. "Hmm, you know what? I think it might be time to take a walk along the waterfront."

Shannon nodded. "Good idea. I'll head back to CCCP and see if I can find confirmation that we can legally prevent anyone from fishing in specific areas."

FIVE

"D id you think there'd be that many of them? I had no idea, Zachary. And look how small they are! It's nothing more than a sardine tin with wings."

"Well, relax. We're not planning on going up in one of those sea planes. But, you're right. There seems to be a lot of them, right? They must have a high demand for them here, or there wouldn't be that many."

Jillian shrugged. "Tourists. I guess that's one way to go fishing. Rent one of those planes and go to some remote area. So, what are we looking for?"

"Someone to talk to," I answered. "We need someone who works on the water. I want to get an idea what the townsfolk really think about our friends at CCCP, hopefully without giving away too much information."

"I guess if we find someone who isn't on

speaking terms with CCCP, then we'd have a lead to investigate," Jillian said.

I nodded. "Exactly. Look, there's a whole row of fishing boats. Maybe we can find someone in there?"

"There are so many. How are we supposed to figure out which one we should approach?"

After a few moments, I came to a stop, which forced my little group to do the same. I pointed at Sherlock and Watson.

"I say we let those two do what they do best: discover the answer for us. Guys? We need a friendly person to talk to, preferably one who won't get tight-lipped on us. What do you say? Think you can help us out?"

Both corgis turned to look up at me. Sherlock snorted once, glanced at his packmate, and then went after an itch in his ear. Finished, he rose to his feet, sniffed noses with Watson, and started pulling us east, on Lincoln Street. We walked by familiar shops, bars, and restaurants. After all, we had just walked along this very street yesterday. We passed a large gift shop and suddenly, Crescent Harbor appeared on our right.

The harbor had quite a collection of potential berths for the locals. Those directly before us were longer, which meant they could handle bigger boats. The largest I could see was a white pleasure craft that was probably in the neighborhood of thirty to forty feet long. Similarly sized vessels lined the pier on either side, with the largest up front and the smallest at the end. The next pier to the left had a similar setup, with slightly smaller piers, vessels, and so on down the line as one progressed farther east. By the time we made it to the seventh pier, we were looking at tiny, two-seater dinghies that were probably no longer than a dozen feet in length.

I was about to ask the dogs what we were doing here, since the harbor was half-empty, and the boats that *were* here looked like they were anything but commercially operated crafts. That's when I felt a couple of tugs. Looking down, I saw that the corgis were both standing perfectly still. In fact, they were watching a small, green vessel approach. It had just passed the sea wall and was slowly cruising along the piers until it came to the sixth pier, second from the end. Whoever was piloting the boat had to be an expert, as the tiny vessel seemingly turned on a dime and then backed in, all without so much as *touching* the mooring posts.

Sherlock and Watson wiggled with excitement. An outside observer would probably think that the dogs were waiting for their owner to return home and I was nothing more than a glorified dog walker. I glanced at Jillian, anxious to see if I should continue humoring the dogs. My wife nodded once and shrugged. All righty then. Let's see who's on that boat.

We slowly crossed the covered walkway leading to the piers and turned left, to head toward number six. As we walked, I gave the dogs a little extra slack in the leash, curious as to what they'd do with the extra maneuverability. What'd they do? Run to the end of their leashes and bark like maniacs at a group of long-tailed ducks, who were just trying to take a break from swimming. The birds squawked angrily as they were forced to dive for cover. Sherlock and Watson stared at the water a few moments before I saw them bunch their muscles.

"Oh, absolutely not. You two can remove that particular thought from your puppy brains. You will *not* be jumping into that water, thank you very much. Sherlock, let it go, pal. They're just ducks. Leave 'em alone."

The owner of the green boat, a thirty-something guy wearing dark green waders, a thick flannel work coat, an orange vest over that, and rubber work gloves, nodded once in our direction and tipped his hat. He made it another few steps when Sherlock and Watson abruptly switched directions and managed to place themselves in his way, forcing him to stop.

"Well, hello there," the man said. His tone spoke volumes. I could tell he was a dog lover, as he seemed genuinely pleased to see the corgis, but I could also tell this poor dude sounded utterly exhausted. "Corgis, eh? You're the second set I've seen this month. Cool dogs, buddy."

"Thanks," I returned. Sherlock and Watson immediately turned to follow their newest fan.

"Excuse me a for a moment, would you?"

The man turned to regard the four of us. "Yes? Is there something I can do for you?"

"You're the owner of that green boat, aren't you? The one with the orange stripe on it?"

The bearded stranger sighed, slid his hat off—revealing a thick head full of brown curls—and frowned.

"Look, I know Crescent is for residential boats. Mine *is* residential. Yeah, I do a little fishin' on the side. It's not a crime. I know, 'cause I've looked it up. Now, if you'll excuse me, I have places to be."

"Hey, hold up," I called, as the stranger angrily brushed by me. "I couldn't care less about what you do with your boat. We're not from Sitka, but PV. Er, Pomme Valley. That's in Oregon."

You would have thought I had just told this guy that my pockets were lined with gold.

"Tourists?"

"Kinda. Listen, I know how strange this is going to sound," I feebly began, "but my dogs are fairly well known for sticking their noses into places they ordinarily shouldn't go. They singled you out and I'm trying to figure out why."

"You're not with Fish and Game?" the bearded man asked, growing more hopeful by the second.

"Nope. I'm Zack Anderson, and this is my wife, Jillian. And before they have a chance to rupture an eardrum, that's Sherlock and Watson, who have taken quite a fascination with you."

A hand was extended.

"Jason Fleischman. Sherlock and Watson. Cool names. You said your dogs are fascinated by me? Can I ask why?"

"We were hoping you'd be able to tell us," Jillian said.

"Hmm, sorry. Nothing interesting ever happens to me. Look, it's nice to meet y'all, but I do have a job to do, so if you'll excuse me?"

"Sorry, pal," I said, stepping to the side and pulling the dogs with me. "I assumed you were coming in from a day of fishing."

Jason looked left, then right. "Between you and me, I was, only all the good spots were spoken for. Whenever I have a crap day, then that means I gotta head to my other job, which is there for emergencies like this."

"If you don't mind me asking, Jason," my wife began, "what do you do?"

"Construction. I got a buddy who runs his own crew. He knows I'm not in the best spot, financially-speaking, and told me anytime I need extra cash, I could always work on his cleanup crew. If I don't work, I don't get paid. I can't go home with no pay, so I have to …"

"… we can hire you," Jillian interrupted.

"… leave now or otherwise I … what did you say?"

"I'd like to hire you," my wife repeated.

"To do what?" Jason wanted to know.

Unsure what Jillian had in mind, I jammed my hands in my pockets and gave her a quizzical look.

"Well, how about some sight-seeing?" she smoothly returned. "You have a boat. How about a quick tour? While we're doing that, we were hoping you could help us out. We are in desperate need of a local's point-of-view, so if you're willing to talk to us, we're willing to pay."

"Umm ..."

"It's nothing illegal," I assured our new friend. "We were hoping to get a local's opinion on the current state of cr ..."

"How much?" Jason interjected.

"Oh. Well, I think we could probably do ..."

"Would five-hundred work?" Jillian interrupted. She opened her purse and pulled out five hundred-dollar bills.

"Five-hundred for a tour and a bit of information," Jason said, in a neutral voice.

Jillian was crestfallen. "Oh, that isn't enough? Well, I could ..."

"Ma'am? For five-hundred bucks, I'd throw my wife in the harbor. In the dead of winter. Along with my first-born, once I have one. So, you're paying for information? What are you, some type of reporter?"

"Do we look like reporters?" I laughed. "Actually, what we're looking for is an outside opinion of how things are with the fishing industry."

Jason scratched at his beard. "Fishing? You want to know about fishing? Erm, okay. What do you wanna know?"

"You mentioned earlier that all the good spots

were taken," Jillian reminded him. "What happens if one fisherman ventures too close to another?"

"In this day and age? World War III. Why? What did you hear? My name wasn't brought up, was it? You're sure you're not with Fish and Game? Or the cops?"

I figured now would be a bad time to bring up the fact that the dogs and I are police consultants back home, so I let that little factoid remain unspoken.

"We aren't," Jillian confirmed. "We're just trying to figure out if anyone around here is, well, angry with …"

"You're with CCCP," Jason accused. "Man, I should've seen this coming. Forget I said anything. I'm outta here."

"No, listen," I pleaded, as I grabbed Jason's arm. "Fine, we'll be honest with you. We don't work for CCCP, but we're here, keeping an eye on them. There have been some, er, threats, regarding that research facility, and after doing a little digging, we were told that we should be looking at the fishermen. Something about CCCP preventing people from fishing in certain areas? Does this make any sense?"

"Keep your voice down," Jason urged. He looked around, as if trying to find a private spot in which he could talk freely. "Come on. Back to my boat. I know just where we can go."

Fifteen minutes later, Jillian and I were huddled together in the boat's tiny wheelhouse. Jason was at the helm, deftly navigating his boat into a tiny cove not ten minutes from Crescent Harbor. Once we were there, he cut the engine and turned to regard us with neutral look.

"This looks like a good spot," Jillian decided.

"For a murder," I quietly mumbled.

Overhearing, Jason burst out laughing, causing the two of us to nearly jump out of our skins. Sherlock and Watson, currently stretched out on a blanket on the floor, looked up at us and woofed a warning.

"Is that what you think of me?" Jason wheezed, between guffaws. "I'm not gonna hurt either of you. Now, some of the dudes I know, I wouldn't put it past them. Okay, we're here. Out with it. What has CCCP done? What's going on?"

I looked at Jillian. "How much do we tell him?"

My wife held out the five hundred-dollar bills.

"He seems nice. I think we can trust him. Jason, are you married?"

"Three years this December."

"Congrats, pal," I told him. "Kids?"

"One on the way. Due in about five weeks. That's why I'm trying to work as much as possible. The crab season has been cancelled, so I'm trying for salmon, only the rest of the guys won't let me anywhere near the good runs. With this level of bullying, you'd think we were back in high school."

"Can't you report them to somebody?" Jillian asked.

"Trust me, that would not go over well.

Everyone would know who turned them in. Besides, I promised Arlen, that'd be my wife, I would stay outta trouble and make an honest day's pay."

Jillian pulled out another five bills.

"Then, we'll make this believable. Let's make it an even thousand. You answer whatever questions we ask, and you promise not to let anyone know we've had this conversation. If anyone asks about today, then you simply say that you were hired by some tourists. Do we have a deal?"

"Absolutely, ma'am. We have a deal. Hey, are you comfortable? Would you like me to make some coffee? I have a little coffee maker over there, or I could ..."

Jillian placed a hand over his.

"Jason. Deep breaths. It's okay. There's no need to make a fuss over us. Now, first question. Do you know many of the other fishermen?"

"All of them," Jason confirmed.

"Do you know if any are angry enough to commit an act of sabotage?" I asked.

Jason's eyes widened. "Something's happened, hasn't it? What's going on? What happened to CCCP?"

I locked eyes with my wife. After a few moments, Jillian nodded.

"There's been a theft," I said. "If we don't find ... let's call it the missing *item*, and get it returned soon, then CCCP is never going to attain its accreditation and will more than likely close up."

"You cannot repeat this to anyone," Jillian ordered.

"I won't," Jason promised. "The new penguin place? It's in danger of closing? What was stolen?"

"Something that should never have left the facility," I said. "Let's leave it at that, okay? So, our question to you is, among the fishermen around here, does anyone have the *cojones* to pull something like that off?"

"*Cojones*," Jason chortled. "Well, let's see. If you wanted me to come up with some names, then on top of that list would be Buck Sherman. He's lived up here his whole life and comes from a long line of fishermen. Thing is … wait. Let me show you something." Our new friend rummaged through a bin next to the boat's helm before coming up with a long tube. He popped off the cardboard stopper and slid out a map. Moving to a small table, he hastily cleared away some dirty dishes and a few handheld tools. "Now, look. We're here. Up there, at the end of Harbor Mountain Road is where you'll find CCCP."

"What water rights do they have?" I asked, as I studied the map. "According to this, the only thing they'd have access to is this section of Granite Creek, running here. That's freshwater, isn't it? Why would your industry be angry with CCCP for buying up those water rights?"

Jason shook his head and traced his finger along the river until it emptied into Sitka Sound.

"I don't know how they managed it, but

somehow, your penguin pals got their grubby mitts on this section of shore here and here. Those are known runs for snow crab and sockeye salmon, two of the most prized catches out there."

"That's what Shannon was talking about," I said. "I guess I don't see why CCCP would need that land. Why buy property right there, away from the complex? If they're planning on going fishing, well, this is the first we've heard about it. These guys are researchers, not fishermen."

"That we know of," Jillian added.

I had to concede the point. Perhaps Dr. Rozhkov hasn't told us everything?

A low rumbling sounded, and for once, it didn't come from the dogs. Jason gave us a sheepish smile.

"Sorry 'bout that. I haven't had anything to eat since breakfast. Do you mind if I have a snack? It'll keep my stomach from complaining."

"Please," Jillian said, giving him a smile, "do help yourself."

"Thanks."

Our seafaring friend opened a small cabinet behind the table and pulled out a tiny cooler. A banana and a bag of chips appeared on the table. This is the part where I say Sherlock and Watson sensed a disturbance in the Force and woke from their nap. In fact, both corgis leapt to their feet while groggily blinking their eyes.

"Morning, Sunshine," I teased.

Sherlock cast me his famous stink-eye look.

Jason eyed the dogs and watched them zero in on the yellow fruit he was holding.

"What's the matter with them? Do they like fruit?"

I studied Sherlock and Watson and noticed they only had eyes for the banana.

"Looking at them, you'd think I starved them on a regular basis. Guys? It's not for you, but for our new friend. Let it go."

Jason took a bite and looked at the dogs, who hadn't blinked—nor moved—since the banana was opened.

"He must really want this banana," Jason decided. "Can they have a piece?"

"Of banana?" I asked. "Sure, it's not going to hurt them. A little piece for each would be fine."

Jason broke off a small section of the fruit and offered it to the dogs. Both corgis stared at him for a few moments more before sitting at his feet. Neither dog made a move for the food.

"What's with you guys?" I demanded. "He's being nice, so … oh! A banana? Really?"

"What is it?" Jillian asked.

"I want to try something. Let me pull out my phone. There. Sherlock, Watson, I took the pic, so would you … and just like that, they're eating."

"What does that tell you?" Jason wanted to know.

"That somehow, this whole mess with CCCP? A banana is involved."

Jason broke out with laughter, but quickly

sobered once he saw that I was serious.

"I'm sorry. I thought you were joking. What does a banana have to do with anything?"

I pocketed my cell and shrugged.

"No clue. That's not the way those two work. I won't go into details, but suffice to say, when they fixate on something, we pay attention. Usually."

"Jason," Jillian said, leaning forward, "the areas you were talking about, near the mouth of this creek? How far does it extend?"

A pen was produced. Jason drew an elongated, somewhat squished oval around an area that, according to the map's key, was nearly a half-mile long.

"From here to there, on both sides." A second mark was made. This one was circular, and was nearly five times the size of the previously marked area. "And this? This area is a known snow crab run. You can see how much area is now covered by CCCP's purchase."

"What about the salmon?" I asked. "You said salmon fishing was also great in that area. Where, specifically?"

Another large circle joined the area. It overlapped the crabbing circle by nearly half, and that included a small area near the shore.

Jillian tapped the map. "If *this* represents those trying to harvest crab, and *that* is the area where salmon can be found, then I'd say there should be plenty of people angry about the loss of that area."

"What happens if someone tries to fish those

waters?" I wanted to know.

"One call," Jason said. "One call to Fish and Game, and your license is revoked."

"No wonder you were afraid of us, back when you thought we were from Fish and Game."

Jason nodded. "Exactly."

"So, let me rephrase that question," I said. "Instead of fishermen, what about the crab guys? Crabbers? Whatever they're called. Can you think of anyone who would be willing to take out their aggression on CCCP?"

"Buster. Buster Ainsworth. He's a hot-headed piece of … I apologize, ma'am. I was about to use foul language."

Jillian hooked a thumb at me.

"I hear it from him all the time."

"You do not," I argued.

"Mm-hmm. Jason, you were saying that you know of some crabbers who might do something foolish?"

Jason sighed, slipped off his wool hat and took a seat at the small table.

"I tried it. Once."

"You tried what?" I asked.

Jillian put a restraining hand on my shoulder.

"Hush. Let him tell his story."

"Right. Sorry."

"It was only the one time," Jason said, continuing on. "Everyone talks about how plentiful the crabs are, and I thought to myself that I should be able to take a piece of that. After all, the industry is good, viable, and very lucrative. I bought myself a few traps and approached some friends of mine to ask which area I could try. You'd think I told everyone I was takin' over. Man alive, what an ordeal that turned out to be."

"Did you ever get a chance to use your traps?" I asked.

In answer to the question, Jason angrily pointed at a couple of shiny, new crab traps. The only thing missing was the price tags.

"All the areas were spoken for," Jillian guessed. "They wouldn't let you place your traps."

"Nope. All unofficial, of course. The boys all learned a long time ago to keep the authorities out of it. If they get involved, then no one wins."

"And the fishing?" I inquired.

"Tiring. I head out at first light and consider it a good day if I can cover fuel costs. Every once in a while, I might get lucky and snag myself a salmon. Doesn't happen often, though."

"Do you enjoy fishing?" I asked.

"Hate it with a passion," Jason returned, without missing a beat. "I hate the smell, the taste, all those little bones, and the fact that I have to rely on them to make a living. Before you say I should consider another line of work, what else am I gonna do around here? It's not like there's an ample supply of jobs."

"What about tourism?" Jillian asked. "You could always offer whale-watching tours around the islands. You probably know them better than anyone."

"You gotta have the right setup for tourists," Jason groaned. "A nice, comfy boat. Coolers for water, or drinks. Maybe even a bathroom. I'm savin' every penny I get just to try and get myself a nice boat. I'll admit, though, at the rate I'm goin', I'll be a grandpa before I see it happen. Oh, well. It don't cost to dream big, does it?"

"Doesn't," I heard my wife whisper.

"What happens if you try dropping your traps anyway?" I asked, growing frustrated for our new friend. "Couldn't you at least give that a try?"

"Everyone knows everybody," Jason groaned. "That's the problem. We know which boat belongs to which guy, so if someone tries to lay a trap somewhere they're not supposed to be, well, all hell breaks loose."

"You mentioned that you work long hours," I recalled. "You spend so many hours out on the water, but then you said you barely break even. Can I ask why? Are the fish becoming scarce?"

"Not at all," Jason countered. "I pull my limit nearly every day of the week. Granted, there are days I don't get a full haul, and when I don't, I feel fortunate to have another job to fall back on."

"The construction job," I said, recalling Jason's explanation from earlier.

"Right."

"So, what's the problem with the fish?" Jillian wanted to know.

"Selling those fish," Jason reported, becoming

glum.

"Don't tell me someone has the clout to make all the restaurants treat a specific person in such a harsh manner?" Jillian said, growing angry.

"No, it's not anything like that," Jason said, shaking his head. "It's the demand. What's the point of buying the fish if there's no way for the restaurants to sell it?"

Comprehension dawned. "Tourism has been hit lately."

"Like you wouldn't believe," Jason confirmed.

"And crabbing would be hit just as hard," Jillian guessed.

"Not as hard, but close," Jason said.

"Couldn't you just switch to catching lobsters?" I asked. "Can you use the same trap?"

Jason shrugged. "You can, sure, but they're more limited in area than the king crab. You see all those boats out there? They should be full of crab right now. But, the season has been cancelled for the second time in a row."

"You've hung out with your friends before, am I right?" I asked, as I turned to Jason.

"Yeah, I suppose. Why?"

"If CCCP wouldn't have purchased the water rights to that area there, on the map, do you think everyone would be fine with them? I mean, after all, they brought jobs to Sitka. They purchased land to breed their penguins. They're paying their bills and buying their supplies here. I doubt very much they're hurting anyone."

Jason was silent for a few moments before nodding. "I get it. You want to talk to a crabber, don't you? Here, let's fire *DeeDee* up and head back to town."

"DeeDee?" I asked.

"My boat. She may not be the youngest girl at the ball, but she'll turn a head or two."

I turned to regard Jason with new respect. "Kudos for that. Well played, pal."

Jason grinned and gave a mock bow.

"What'd I miss?" Jillian wanted to know.

I pointed at Jason. "He just quoted a line from *Down Periscope*. I *love* that movie!"

"You've watched it?" Jason asked. He bumped my fist. "Right on, man. Sometimes, it gets lonely on the water. I got a TV and a VHS player over there, with about twenty movies. It helps pass the time."

We were slowly cruising along the shore, heading toward town, when Jason pointed.

"Crescent Harbor, dead ahead."

The rumbling of the boat's motor awakened the corgis, who had just drifted off after their banana snack. Sherlock rolled to his feet, stretched his back, and then—and only then—rose to his feet. Watson was already waiting for him. The two of them looked at me, then at Jillian, and then turned to watch Jason at the controls of the boat. Sherlock watched for a few moments when his nose suddenly lifted. Both he and Watson executed a tight turn and trotted through the open cabin door, which led to the stern of the ship. Both corgis approached the unused crab traps, sniffed a few times, then moved off. Sherlock went left, while Watson turned right. Both sniffed along the deck until they hit the boat's bulwark. Since *DeeDee* wasn't that big, it was only a matter of time before the two corgis came face-to-face with each other. However, what they found had us three humans staring, mouths agape.

The dogs had stopped at a small *something*, which had become lodged in a loose plank at the upper edge of the gunwale. Curious to see what it was, Jason gently pried the item free. He stared at the object for a few moments before shrugging and then tossing it into an open box by the cabin's door.

"Sorry, nothing to see here. It's just a toy."

Did I actually see what I thought I did? Noticing the dogs were now watching the bin, as though they expected the toy to make a return appearance at any moment, I retrieved the item and held it up.

"Don't worry 'bout that," Jason told me. We had just turned at the sixth pier and our captain was preparing to dock his boat. "Arlen and I had some friends over last week. Their little boy was with him. I didn't realize he left that thing behind."

I held the toy up for Jillian to see.

It was a stuffed dragon.

SIX

T his really isn't what I had in mind," I told
my wife, several hours later. It was now
two in the afternoon, and we were on board yet
another boat. This time, it was a small whale-
watching vessel, having set off on our mini-
adventure fifteen minutes ago. It was just the four
of us, since Shannon was still tied up with CCCP,
and consequently informed us via text that she'd
be preoccupied for the next several hours.

We had wanted to check into the local crabbing
industry, only what we discovered was the
crabbers were a very tight-lipped bunch. No one
was willing to talk with us, and no one certainly
wanted to go on record to talk about the new
research facility that had moved to the area *and*
stolen some of their prime crabbing grounds.

Jillian spent the next hour or so on her phone.
I've seen her get preoccupied like that before, and
that typically meant she had something up her
sleeve. But, every time I asked her what she was
doing, she'd give me a coy smile and assure me

that I'd find out later. What she *did* do was manage to find something to do which covered all of our bases.

I'm sure right about now you're thinking, *explain yourself, Zack.* No problem, let me give you some context.

We knew we needed to approach some crabbers, and we also knew that they'd more than likely refuse to talk to us. But, I also knew if we could find the right circumstances, I would be willing to wager I could convince one of them to open up. And when it came to the locals, Jillian found the perfect solution: cold, hard cash.

No, it's not what you think. We didn't bribe anyone. However, with this town hurting as much as it had been when the cruise industry was shut down, we knew people would more than likely turn the other way when money would switch hands. So, in this case, Jillian found an excursion popular among the cruisers for us to attend, where, after a wildlife tour around the smaller islands, our little adventure would culminate with a visit to a private island and a succulent snow crab dinner. Since we wanted to talk to someone about the crabbing industry, we figured this would be a great way to do it. Plus, there was outdoor seating, away from the kitchen. That meant we could bring the dogs. Oh, did I mention the name of where we're going? Ainsworth Island Lodge. Yep, *that* Ainsworth. Jillian is *that* good when it comes to uncovering juicy little tidbits online. As for me, well, I'm figuring that someone on that teeny, tiny little island is related to the Buster Ainsworth who Jason had mentioned.

"I hope we see some whales," Jillian said. She was wearing her heavy winter coat, buttoned all the way up to her throat, and had her soft, purple scarf wrapped around her neck a few times. "Personally, I don't think we saw enough the last time we were up here."

"At least, you saw some," I chuckled. My outer wear consisted of a simple black sweatshirt with a very recognizable dwarf on the back. And if you're wondering, yes, it's the same one I was wearing before. "All I saw was a couple of snorts of air as the whales came up to breathe. By the time I got the camera pointed in the right direction, they were long gone."

We felt the boat slow. Then the engine shut off, allowing us to coast to a stop.

"What are we doing?" Jillian asked. "Is there something out there?"

I unzipped my backpack and retrieved the binoculars. Once I looked west, I saw the reason why we stopped. Jillian, I noticed, was looking in the wrong direction.

Reaching up, I hooked a finger under her chin and gently turned her head left.

"See those bobbing dots in the water, about three hundred feet away?"

"Yes. What are they?"

I handed her the binoculars.

"Take another look."

"Oh! Otters! A raft of them!"

The fuzzy critters were reclining on their backs in close proximity to one another. Our guide explained it was for the protection of the group, but thanks to our time in Monterey, we already knew this. We each took some pictures, and I shot some video as we gently drifted by.

Next up were bald eagle nests. Tons of them. Everywhere we looked, it seemed, we spotted nesting eagles. Some weren't that far above the water. Others seemingly chose to get as high as possible. On more than one occasion, we watched those majestic birds glide over the water, swipe at the surface with a claw, and come away with a writhing fish almost half as large as they were. Sea lions surfaced every ten minutes or so, making me think the sleek creatures were following along behind us, hoping for a handout.

We had actually reached the turning point, which signaled it was time to start toward the island, when our luck improved. Significantly. Sherlock, who had been sitting contentedly next to me on the boat's observation deck, perked up. He sniffed the air a few times and then turned to look at me, as if he was waiting for me to identify the scent he had just smelled. As for Watson, she was more interested in watching me than the abundant wildlife that was everywhere we looked. However, my little girl suddenly lifted her nose, inhaled, and let out a whine.

"What is it, guys?"

A spray of water erupted at the same time I felt the motor shut off. There, less than twenty feet away, a large male humpback whale was resting just below the surface of the water. Apparently, it had just decided to surface and take a breath. Granted, we weren't allowed to get any closer, but it really wasn't necessary. As we drifted by, we all watched as the whale's head turned to regard us. The huge cetacean must have decided we were harmless since he slipped beneath the surface, but was still visible as he (probably) went back to sleep, or whatever they do.

I looked over at Jillian, to see what she thought of the encounter when I saw her holding her phone up, taking pictures. Oh, son of a biscuit eater. I was that close to a whale and didn't even *think* about snapping a few shots.

"Good for you. I, uh, forgot."

"Forgot what? To take pictures? You're in luck, Zachary. There's another! And another! Oh, my! Look, it's a pod! They're everywhere!"

Man, I don't know how much the tour company was paying this boat captain, but he earned his money today. We had quite literally stumbled into the middle of a large group of humpbacks. I saw several mothers with their calves. Adults, juveniles, it didn't matter. They were all there. We were told the juvenile males were the ones venturing close to the boat, no doubt curious as to what we were.

I heard another whine coming from the dogs. Sherlock and Watson were on their feet and straining to look over the edge of the boat to see the whales that much better. Watson sidled up to me, whined piteously, and turned her woeful eyes up at me.

"What's the matter, girl?" I asked, growing concerned. "Are you feeling seasick? Are you … wait. You want me to lift you up, don't you? Seriously?"

Sighing, I scooped up Watson and held her close to my chest. My little girl's nose was sniffing so fast it felt like a mini leaf blower against my skin. Her ears were pointing straight up, her nub of a tail was happily wagging, and her eyes were open so wide that it almost looked like she was going to give me what I called her *psycho eyes*. Most dog owners will back me up. Give your fur babies one of their favorite treats, and just before they take it, look at their eyes. Typically, they'll be open so wide that you'll be able to see the whites of their eyes. That's what Watson was giving me now.

"*Awwoooo,*" Sherlock complained.

"Is it your turn? Fine. Jillian, would you take Watson's leash? Okay, thanks. Sherlock—up you go. There. What do you think?"

One of the whales chose that moment to literally swim right next to the ship. Sensing Sherlock might like to get a little closer, I took him down to the main level of the boat and approached the water's edge. The whale was there, and I was absolutely floored by what I saw. The huge marine mammal had gently rolled until one of its massive eyes was just below the surface. The huge orb blinked once and then fixated on Sherlock.

The tri-colored corgi stretched forward as far as he could as he stared at the strange behemoth in the water. I'm sure the inquisitive little corgi had never sniffed noses with a whale before, so this particular scent must be utterly fascinating for him. Sherlock kept turning to me, back to the whale, and then back to me, as if he was checking to see if I was looking at the same thing.

"They're big, aren't they?"

Jillian arrived at my side. Together, the four of us stood in silence and watched the majestic creatures surface, take a huge gulp of air, and then dip below the waves, only to reappear a few minutes later in a different spot. Watson turned to me, craned her neck to make eye contact, and then proceeded to lick my hand.

"Come here, girl." I returned to the seats we had occupied on the ride out and sat down. Since the boat had only been about a third of the way full, there was room for the dogs to jump up on the bench beside us and settle down. I wrapped a protective arm around Jillian and, together, we all sat in silence for a few moments. "They're fantastic creatures, aren't they?"

"They're wonderful," Jillian said, snuggling close. "We never got to see them like this last time."

"No, we didn't."

"Ladies and gentlemen," an announcement began, over the ship's PA system, *"we will arrive at Ainsworth Island Lodge in ten minutes. I do hope you've enjoyed spending some time with us. And, I hope you brought your appetite, because supper is ready and waiting for us. Just sit back, enjoy the ride, and if you're suffering from a chill in the air, hot beverages are available at the back of the boat. Please help yourselves. Tips and donations are always welcomed. Thank you and we hope you had a wonderful time."*

Ainsworth Island is a small, private island that is less than ten acres in size. It contains walkways along both the north and south beaches. A ringside fire allowed visitors to sit outside and enjoy their meal, if they chose. Consequently, that was where the four of us sat, seeing how we had the dogs with us and I really didn't want to press my luck by trying to sneak them inside the lodge.

I took the dogs' leashes and selected a picnic table near the fire. Jillian retreated into the lodge to grab herself a plate of food from the buffet-style offerings. I opened my backpack, pulled out three small bowls, and fed both dogs. Moments later, I filled the third bowl with water and set it next to them.

"You're going to have a field day in there," Jillian reported, as she set her plate of food next to mine. "They've got crab legs, prime rib, grilled wild salmon, steamed collard greens, and mashed potatoes and gravy. There are also fixings for a salad, fresh home-made rolls, and a small bar, in case you wanted a beer. Here, give me the leashes. Get yourself something to eat. Have the dogs eaten?"

Surprised, I looked down at the three bowls. Two were empty and one had a several inches of water left. Wow. That was fast, even for Watson. Since when did Sherlock wolf down his food? Then I looked at Jillian's plate and chuckled. The canny little stinker was hoping he'd be able to sneak a morsel or two from us. No wonder he ate so fast.

Once I had made my selections, and I had my bottle of soda next to my food, we dug in. Trust me, eating crab, in Alaska, cooked by those who obviously know how to make it—it doesn't get any better than this.

Seated next to the fire, talking and laughing, and playing with the dogs, encouraged several of the other tourists to join us, too. We officially met the Johnson family, of Chicago. This family of six consisted of the parents (in their late twenties) and four kids, ranging in age from four to twelve years of age. All the kids, I might add, absolutely adored the dogs.

We still had another half an hour to kill here on this pristine island, and since it was warm enough outside, we elected to stay at our table. A matronly woman approached us with a bottle of beer in her hand. She had shoulder-length gray hair pulled into a pony tail, and then clipped to the back of her head like I've seen many others do. She had a weathered face, no doubt from years spent in the sun, sparkling blue eyes, was wearing a wide smile, and had on a dark gray tee shirt (advertising the lodge) with a pair blue jeans. Steel-toed work boots completed the picture. The woman raised her bottle in greeting and gave us an inquiring look. Jillian nodded first.

"Come, join us. I don't remember seeing you on the boat. Are you someone who works here?"

"Beverly Ainsworth. I own the lodge, and this island. Thank you so much for coming out to visit us."

"You own this place?" I said, sweeping an arm in a circle. "You must love it here. It's so quiet, and peaceful."

"Serene," Jillian added.

I held up my fist. "Nice word, my dear."

My wife and I bumped fists. Beverly noticed and smiled warmly at the two of us.

"So, who do we have here?" she politely asked.

"I'm Zack. This is my wife, Jillian. We ..."

"WOOOOOOF!" Sherlock protested.

"You have no one to blame but yourself for that," Jillian teased. "He knew you weren't going to introduce him next."

I waited a few moments for the ringing in my ears to stop.

"Sorry. I haven't done that in a while. Down there, with the very impressive set of canine lungs, is Sherlock. Over there, enjoying the warmth of the fire, is ..."

"Omigod! If you say that one's name is Watson, then I'm probably going to pass out."

I don't know what caused me to say the following, but I'll just chalk it up to being in a good mood.

"Well, have a seat, sister. Her name is, indeed, Watson."

Beverly gasped and sank down on an empty spot on the opposite side of our table. I then felt a light swat on my shoulder.

"Sister?" Jillian repeated, giggling.

I shrugged. "I don't know. It just came out."

"I can't believe it," Beverly was saying. "Y-you guys … you're all famous!"

"I wouldn't go that far," I protested.

"Were you, or were you not, on television, getting married in England?" Beverly argued. "I seem to recall seeing the Queen of England in attendance at your wedding, or did my eyes fail me?"

At a loss for what to say, I looked to Jillian for help. My darling wife just smiled at me and let me continue to flail about.

"Okay, that might have been us."

"And Sherlock and Watson? Were they the ones who found that missing jewelry?"

"On more than one occasion," I said, nodding.

"It's not often we get celebrities here," Beverly said, pleased. "Before you leave, you'll have to let us take your picture. We'll put it on our Wall of Fame in the gift shop."

"Oh, you don't need to do that," Jillian said.

"And I won't, if you really don't want me to," Beverly returned. Her smile widened. "But, I'm hoping I can persuade you otherwise. What brings you fine folks to my island?"

"Anything with the word *crab* in the menu will typically get my attention," I said, trying to sound as blasé as possible.

Both Jillian and Beverly laughed.

"I'd ask if you're on a cruise," the island's owner began, "but I know you're not. It's too late in the year for cruisers to be hitting these parts. That means you came up, on your own. It snowed yesterday, it's mostly gone now, thank goodness, but I can tell more snow is in the air. I'd give it three days before we'll be waist deep in it. Therefore, something *else* brought you out here. Oh, heavens above. Tell me you're not here for my son. Tell me this has nothing to do with Buster."

Hoo, boy. I should've seen this coming.

With a huff, Beverly stood.

"I'm not going to let you smear his good name over something so trivial. You're a paying guest, so I won't make you go, but I don't …"

"Just a moment," I interrupted, holding my hands up in a time-out gesture. "No one is accusing anyone of anything. I've personally never met your son."

"What trivial act are you referring to?" Jillian asked.

"You   tell   me.   You're   the   one   slinging

accusations."

"I was doing nothing of the sort," I argued. "Look, I was talking about whatever you're accusing him of, that's all. Look, we just want to talk. Hear us out. If you don't like anything you hear, just say so, okay? We'll change the subject."

"Then, change the subject *now*," Beverly ordered.

"Hear what we have to say first," I insisted. "Then, I'll be more than happy to talk about whatever subject you'd like."

"Fine. Whadya want?""

"We're all friends here," I urged. "First off, I think you should know we're not accusing Buster of anything."

"Bull," Beverly argued. "And if what you say is true, then why are you here?"

I pointed at the dogs. "You're familiar with Sherlock and Watson, right?"

"I am. What about it? Are you saying they led you to me?"

"Er, no."

"Your dogs have insinuated Buster is guilty of something?"

I shook my head. "As a matter of fact, no. Wait. Your son, does he go by any nicknames? Maybe moose, or dragon, or, uh, banana?"

"Banana?" Beverly repeated. Much of her anger evaporated. "That's a new one on me. I'm sorry. I shouldn't have snapped at you people. However, there's only so much grief a parent can stomach when it comes to your children."

"Has Buster been causing you problems?" Jillian asked.

"Since the day that boy was born," Beverly told us. "He's a good boy, only he's got a short temper. He means well, I know he does, only ..."

"... it's hard to defend when he acts so pigheaded," my wife finished.

"Exactly. Got a kid like that?"

"We don't, no," Jillian said, shaking her head.

"That's too bad. Want one of mine?"

I snorted with laughter. At least, I hoped she was joking.

"Just level with me," Beverly urged. "What's he done?"

"We don't have any evidence he's done anything wrong," I assured her. "However, we were given his name as a possible suspect."

"Suspect? What do you suspect he's done?"

"Where was your son earlier this week?"

"*This* week?" Beverly repeated. "Washington. He's helping a friend of his, so he'll be out of town for at least a couple of weeks. This friend of his needed an extra pair of hands on his boat. He's a fisherman, and my Buster is one of the best. I don't expect him back anytime soon. Is that what you needed to know?"

"And there's no chance he's here now?" I asked.

"None," Beverly confirmed.

Jillian and I shared a look. "Well, that rules him out."

Sherlock and Watson both looked up, in unison. Noticing, Beverly watched them for a few moments.

"What's with them?"

"That's a damn good question," I admitted. "Guys? What's the matter? Do you smell something?"

As one, the corgis faced north. Both ears were sticking straight up and their noses were going a mile a minute. I personally hadn't heard anything approach, but those two clearly smelled something.

A long, drawn out moan sounded, lasting at least fifteen seconds. It was loud, it was powerful, and it sounded like it came from the same direction as the dogs were looking. A second call started. This time, it lasted less than five seconds, and if I wasn't mistaken, the call sounded shrill. What in the world could it be?

"No sudden moves," Beverly began, as she slowly got to her feet. "I mean that. No sudden movement. Keep a good hold of those leashes, you got me?"

"What's going on?" I asked, growing concerned. I placed myself between Jillian and the dogs. "Is it a bear?"

"It's worse," Beverly confirmed. I could only hope she was joking, but judging by her dead-pan face, whatever it was that made the noise was not a welcome addition to her island, and was most certainly not included in the itinerary for today's events.

We felt the thump before we heard it. Then there was another. My eyes widened as I realized what I was hearing: footfalls. Something large was on the island with us, and whatever it was, it was coming closer.

"Tell me you guys don't have any yetis on this island."

Beverley smiled briefly.

"No, 'fraid not."

"Zachary, look! It's a moose!"

Out of nowhere, a huge adult moose appeared. I was about to ask whether or not this was a male or female, but then I spotted two spindly-legged calves exploring the lapping water on the beach. The mother grazed on a patch of grass near a fallen log while keeping her offspring in sight.

"A cow and two young 'uns," Beverly said, appearing on my right.

"This is an island," I pointed out. "How did that mother, with those two little babies, make it out here? Can they swim?"

"A moose can swim just fine," Beverly confirmed. "However, those babies are too young to attempt a crossing. That's why they would have crossed just over there."

I shaded my eyes. "What are we looking at?"

"Look north, which is *that* way," I was instructed.

"There's nothing but water there," I told her.

"Yes, there's water, but it's only about two feet

deep at the moment. I'll wager they crossed there."

The two calves nosed at the grass a few times, no doubt curious as to why their mother kept placing her snout on the ground for extended periods of time. One calf managed to tear off a mouthful of grass, but then didn't know what to do with it. For several long minutes, the youngster froze in place, with grass blades hanging out of its mouth.

The mother emitted another call. This time, it lasted for just a few seconds, but it had the desired effect. The calf with the mouthful of grass spit it out and hurried as quickly as it could to make it by her mother's side. The second calf was splashing through the water, but quickly abandoned its playtime. Together, the threesome headed north. The cow moose waded into the water, checked once to see if she was being followed, and headed off.

Sherlock and Watson, I should point out, had also frozen in place. In fact, neither one of them moved a muscle, with the exception of sitting down directly where they were. That explained why I had a corgi sitting on one of my shoes, and another sitting by my leg.

Realizing this was yet another moose corgi clue, I snapped a few photos of the moose family, not just because it was part of the case, but because we were less than fifty feet from a huge, wild animal. That mother moose was probably at least six-hundred pounds.

"Majestic animals, aren't they?" Beverly said,

breaking all of us out of our trances.

"They're huge," I agreed.

"That was a female, if you couldn't tell by the presence of her babies."

I nodded. "I gathered as much. How big do they get?"

"That one was probably over eight-hundred pounds. The males can get nearly twice that. On average, I'd say between fourteen-hundred and fifteen-hundred pounds. If you ever encounter an angry bull moose, I would definitely recommend you head the other direction."

I nodded. "Point taken."

Jillian cleared her throat. "Beverly? Can I ask you something?"

"Go ahead."

"Do you know of anyone by the name of Moose? Or, maybe their nickname is Moose?"

"I sure don't. Why do you ask?"

I pointed at the dogs.

"You know who they are, and you know what they're capable of doing. That moose family— that was the third time the dogs have fixated on something pertaining to a moose. We saw one on the side of the road after first arriving here, and we saw a moose crossing sign. Now this."

"This is Alaska," Beverly pointed out. "You'll find moose everywhere."

"Yeah, but did you see those two sitting? That's what they do when they want me to pay attention."

The owner of Ainsworth Island looked at Jillian, no doubt for confirmation I wasn't off my rocker. My wife shrugged and eventually nodded.

"I know it sounds weird, and neither of us has ever been able to figure out how they can do what they do, but the simple fact of the matter is somehow, in some way, we need to be paying attention to the word *moose*."

Beverly placed a friendly hand on my arm.

"If it means that much to you, I can always check the phone book for you. I have one back in my office. Don't go anywhere."

"A phone book," I chuckled. "How archaic. Seems like it wasn't that long ago that consulting a phone book was the ultimate way to research an individual."

"I think I saw somewhere that New York City just removed its very last working phone booth," Jillian recalled.

"Poor Superman," I laughed. "What's this world coming to? Now what's he supposed to use?"

My wife playfully swatted my arm. We looked up to see Beverly walking back to us, holding what had to be the thinnest, smallest phone book I have ever seen. She took a seat next to me.

"Okay, you're looking for someone with the first name of Moose? Let's see."

Jillian and I fell silent as we watched the island's owner skim through the pages. Were we on the right track? Could it be as simple as finding someone with the right name? The corgis were both resting on the ground. The grass was sparse, and looked cold, but neither corgi seemed to mind. Looking slowly around at the surrounding environment, I could see how this type of living would appeal to many. After all, there was no noise. No sounds of passing cars. No airplanes flying overhead, with the exception of a sea plane every hour or so. It was easy to believe that technology didn't exist here.

"Sorry, I don't see anyone by that name. Did you want to see for yourself?"

"I can double-check you," Jillian said, taking the phone book. "Although, if you didn't find anything, I doubt I will, too."

Ten minutes later, we gave up.

"Well, it was a good thought," I said, feeling disappointed. "Besides, I think we all knew it wasn't going to be that easy. It never is with those two."

"Let me see if I have this straight," Beverly began, "we know Sherlock and Watson can find missing jewelry. Have they found missing people before?"

"Yes," I confirmed.

"And your dogs always manage to point you in the right direction?"

Jillian nodded. "Every time."

"And your only clue is a moose?"

I let out the breath I had been holding.

"Well, there's also bananas, dragons, and … shoot. What was the last thing? I know there were four. Or five. Wow, I can't remember."

"Drugs," Jillian answered. "That's what's missing. Or medication, or perhaps pharmacies. Remember that little apothecary shop?"

I snapped my fingers. "Right. I forgot about it."

"Apothecaries," Beverly repeated. "We didn't check for business names. May I have that back, please? Thank you."

Another single-engine sea plane buzzed by overhead. It was low enough to allow us to see the faces of several tourists, plastered against the windows. I felt a nudge on my shoulder and saw that the corgis were looking up at the plane. I was going to blow it off when I noticed both were already in a down position. Worth noting?

"What the hell," I mumbled. I pulled out my cell and snapped another picture. I also noticed neither dog broke their down. Because they chose to or because that plane was never a clue in the first place. Who could say?

"Yes!" Beverly exclaimed. "Look at this! What do you see, right there?"

I took the phone book and, with Jillian leaning over my shoulder, saw for ourselves what she had found. Moose Pharmaceuticals. I do believe fortune was finally smiling on us.

SEVEN

Fortune was smiling at us? Pssht. Whoever came up with that phrase should be shot. It certainly wasn't smiling at me. On the contrary, I think it's been giving us the bird, and by that, I mean, one of the flightless variety. Moose Pharmaceuticals? It's defunct. It went out of business two years ago. But, just for kicks and giggles, we decided to go by the address where the drug store used to reside.

It was now a jewelry store.

And the dogs? They fell asleep in the back of Shannon's car. Sherlock and Watson snoozed on as we drove by the former business, and didn't bother cracking an eye open when we stopped so I could get out for a better look. I think it's safe to say that Moose Pharmaceuticals was just a freak coincidence.

"What about the person who owned it?"

Shannon asked, after I returned to the van. "Maybe we should be focusing on the person rather than the business?"

"We already thought of that," I glumly reported. "Or, more like, *she* did."

"Mr. Jahan Narayan," Jillian read, looking at her phone's display. "Passed away two years ago. No immediate family. The shop was put up for sale, but there were no interested parties. It says here the property was sold nearly four months later, to one Alexandre Deschamps. He turned it into a jewelry store."

"Now *him* I know," Shannon said, smiling. "He's a bachelor who doesn't like to cook. Or doesn't know how, I guess."

"How do you know this?" Jillian wanted to know.

"I don't eat out that often, but it seems like I'm always bumping into him wherever I go."

Interested, I reached for my notebook. "Really? Wouldn't that behavior be reminiscent of a ... I don't know, a stalker?"

"You've got it all wrong," Shannon assured me. "He's one of the nicest guys I've ever met."

"How long has he been living in Sitka?" I asked.

"Ten years, at least."

I looked at Jillian. "Well, scratch that. I don't know, my dear. I'm starting to think we're barking up the wrong tree." Both corgis turned to look at me. Sherlock even had the gall to head-tilt me. "No offense, guys. We're still trying to link everything together. Go back to sleep. What if we're going about this all wrong? What if … what if fishing, or crabbing, has nothing to do with it?"

"But, moose and bananas do?" Shannon argued.

"Push that aside for now," I ordered. "I think we need to come at this from a new angle."

"Such as?" Jillian asked, batting her eyes.

I placed a hand over her eyes, blocking them from view, and continued.

"I'm thinking we should start looking at all businesses who have failed in the last year or so."

My wife sobered. She pulled my hand off her face, gave it a quick peck, and then smiled.

"You have an idea, don't you? Let's hear it."

I cleared my throat. "Well, someone is clearly not a fan of CCCP. We were thinking that it had to be someone who was unhappy about the water rights Dr. Rozhkov was given."

Sherlock lifted his head to watch me from his spot in the cargo area. Why did I suddenly get the impression I was being judged? Was the little booger waiting for me to say something foolish?

"Where should we go from here?" Shannon wanted to know.

Suddenly, an idea loomed. I looked at Shannon, met her eyes in the mirror, and smiled. Then, I took my wife's hand.

"Head to our cabin, would you? We'll drop the dogs off, give them a few treats, and let them take a nap. Then, let's go out to eat. Shannon, would you see if Dr. Rozhkov wants to come along?"

Our guide nodded. "Sure. Where should I tell her to meet us?"

"Pick the best restaurant in town," Jillian suggested. "And we'll be the ones picking up the tab. Zachary, what do you have in mind?"

I waited until Shannon was on the phone with Marianne. As soon as she was, I turned to my wife and dropped my voice.

"We have less than two days left to locate that chick," I began. "Personally, I don't think we've made too much progress, aside from being able to rule out the local fishermen and the crabbers. So, guess what time it is?"

Jillian smiled. "It's time to go over the corgi clues, isn't it?"

"It is. And, the more eyes we have on them, the better."

"We should ask Jason and his wife to join us," Jillian said. "I liked him. I'd like to see him again."

I gave her an expectant glance.

"Does this have something to do with that phone call you made after we made it back to the cabin yesterday? I know you were on the phone for nearly a half hour."

Jillian gave me a coy smile.

"Maybe."

"What are you thinking?" I asked.

"Nothing, really. You'll see."

I shrugged.

"Well, I think I could probably find a number for him online, but I just realized that you probably already thought of that and are several steps ahead of me."

The demure smile was back.

"Maybe. Let's see if I just so happen to have his number." A number was dialed and the phone was placed next to her ear. "Hello? Would this be Arlen? No, you don't know me. We know your husband, though. We were hoping we could invite you and Jason to ... what's that? As a matter of fact, I *am* Jillian. Yes, Zachary is my husband. Anyway, we were ... you're more than welcome. Your husband was very sweet, and we appreciated his help. That's actually what I'm calling about. We were hoping you two could help us again. I wanted to take everyone out to eat and I don't know where to ... oh, thank you very much. Well, could you recommend a place to go? And I'm going to tell you this right now. This is our treat, and don't even think about arguing. If you're helping us, then I'm picking up the tab. There will be no negotiating. So, where might we go? The Eastmark Sitka? They have crab by the pound? My husband is now drooling. Yes, that'll do nicely. Thank you. Let's plan on meeting there this evening, say six o'clock? Perfect. We'll see you then."

By the time Jillian hung up the phone, Shannon was done with her phone call, too.

"Dr. Rozhkov would love to come. And you chose Eastmark Sitka?"

"Arlen did. She says the crab legs there are to die for."

"She's got my vote," I said.

"And Arlen is …?"

"Jason's wife," Jillian answered.

"And Jason is …?" Shannon asked. She and Jillian had locked eyes in the rearview mirror.

"Oh, I'm sorry. Jason is the name of the fisherman we talked to yesterday."

"Ah."

"Did you tell Dr. Rozhkov what time we're meeting?" I wanted to know.

Shannon nodded. "I did."

* * *

That evening, the four of us—Shannon, Dr. Rozhkov, myself, and Jillian—stepped out of one of CCCP's company vans at the Eastmark Sitka restaurant. Turns out our dinner plans were at the onsite restaurant of a local hotel. Eastmark Sitka is located in the heart of downtown. According to the brochure I picked up, this hotel offers over one-hundred different rooms, with top-of-the-line amenities. And, according to Jillian, we were to meet the Fleischmans in the Black Bird Dining Room. It was one of the two restaurants the hotel managed. I snuck a glance at the menu as we walked by and started grinning. All I had to see was the first option under the entrees and I knew we had made the right choice.

Jason and his wife were already waiting for us. The two of them quickly stood as our group approached. Our new friend had cleaned up quite well. His beard had been trimmed, and from the dampness of his hair, I'd say he was freshly showered, too. He was wearing a long-sleeved flannel shirt and a pair of black pants.

Arlen was an attractive, slim brunette with shoulder-length curly black hair. She was wearing a black sequined blouse and black slacks. As we neared, I could see that she was nervously twisting her purse in her hands. What she had to be worried about, I didn't know, aside from looking like she was going to pop at any time. Arlen was pregnant, and if I recalled correctly, the baby was due in just over a month.

After the introductions were made, and everyone ordered their drinks, Jason leaned forward and grinned at both of us.

"I can't thank you enough for hiring me yesterday. Any time you need more information, if I have it, it's yours."

"It means a lot," Arlen shyly added.

"Your husband would make a great tour guide," Jillian said, giving the younger woman a smile. "I think he missed his calling."

"I've been trying to tell him that for years," Arlen admitted. "He won't believe me, of course."

"Jason, I have a question for you," Jillian began, as she put her menu down and turned to face him. "If you had the opportunity and the means, would you want to get out of the fishing industry? Would you want to lead tourists to all the places worth seeing around here?"

Our new friend didn't blink.

"In a heartbeat. I think I might've told you, I *hate* fishing."

"What would you do with your boat?" Jillian politely inquired.

Jason blinked a few times.

"Huh? What about my boat? I'm not getting rid of it, if that's what you're thinking. And no, tourists aren't gonna want to take tours on *DeeDee*."

Having an idea where she was going with this, especially after that phone call yesterday, I took a long drink from my soda and leaned back in my chair. Dr. Rozhkov, or Marianne, as I was ordered to call her tonight, caught my eye. She looked at Jillian and raised an eyebrow. Suddenly, I knew Marianne knew about Jillian's history. Then again, for all I knew, Jillian might have donated some capital to get CCCP open in the first place.

"I'm asking you if you no longer needed your boat, er, *DeeDee*, what would you do with it?"

"Sell it, of course," Arlen said. When her husband looked sharply at her, as if offended, she blushed. "I'm sorry. I hate that boat. It smells."

Jason was silent a few moments, making me think he was going to take the comment as an insult. Thankfully, he grinned and shrugged.

"It's okay. I'm not really fond of it, either. Ma'am, why do you ask? You don't … you don't want to buy her, do you?"

"I don't," Jillian confirmed. "But, I should tell

you that you're not going to need her for much longer. Oh, let's see. I'm trying to remember how long the dealership said it was going to take to deliver her."

"Deliver *who*?" Jason asked, perplexed. He looked at his wife, who looked just as helpless as he did.

"Did you do what I *think* you did?" I casually asked my wife.

Jillian gave me a dazzling smile. "Maybe."

"I don't understand," Jason was saying. "What did you do?"

"You're now the proud owner of a thirty-six foot Newton glass-bottom boat. They're currently doing a bit of customizing, so it'll take a little time to be finished. They're going to enclose the cabin, and install a few optional extras, making certain you'll have everything you need for when you start taking tourists out to sea."

"You w-what?" Jason stammered. "Ma'am? There's absolutely no way I'm ..."

Jillian held a finger to her lips. Jason fell silent immediately. Arlen, surprised by the speed in which her husband closed his mouth, leaned forward.

"Mrs. Anderson? You have *got* to share what magic you just used on him. I've never seen him go quiet as fast as he just did. You bought him a boat?"

"As a way of saying thanks," Jillian said.

"And how much was it?" Jason wanted to know. "I've got to be able to help pay. I think I can get several thousand for *DeeDee*, so ..."

"You'll do nothing of the sort," Jillian interrupted. "It's something nice I'm doing for you. For your family. Now, I'll send you the number of the seller, who's currently in Louisiana, by the way. He's expecting your call tomorrow to arrange shipping. Again, it's all on me."

Jason's shocked eyes met mine.

"Hey, she does stuff like that all the time," I said, shaking my head. "She enjoys helping others. She has the means, she has the motive, and she has the *ire*, should you choose to argue."

Marianne snorted with amusement.

Arlen's eyes filled with tears. Jason looked down and blinked furiously, trying to clear his eyes without wiping them. Arlen took the tissue Jillian offered and gently dabbed her husband's eyes.

"What do you say, my love?"

Jason blinked a few more times. "Th-thank you. I don't know what I did to deserve that, but I'll never forget it. How can I ever repay you?"

I watched my wife ponder the question, but I think she did that just for show. Her answer was too quick; an answer had probably been long thought out.

"*DeeDee*. When you get your new boat, pay it forward. Give *DeeDee* to someone who could truly use her."

"I know just the person," Jason said. He quickly wiped the back of a hand across his face.

"Mark?" Arlen guessed.

Jason nodded.

"He's a friend of ours," Arlen explained. "He helps Jason out from time to time. He's a sweet kid, just out of high school. He knows his way around boats and just wants to help his family."

"That sounds perfect," Jillian decided.

"That was very generous of you," Shannon whispered, who happened to be seated on my left.

Jillian shrugged. "Zachary is right. I enjoy helping people."

"I'll say," Dr. Rozhkov agreed.

Shannon turned to give her boss a questioning look before turning to Jillian.

"It was you. You funded CCCP."

"I am one of the principle investors," Jillian confirmed.

Shannon looked at me.

"Did you know about this?"

"Nope."

Shannon's eyes widened.

"And this doesn't bother you?"

"Not in the slightest," I confirmed. "My wife is an absolute whiz when it comes to finances and crunching numbers. She enjoys helping others open businesses. In fact, I think she probably owns half the town where we live. But, she's someone who'll never gloat about it, or rub it in your face. She's that kindhearted."

Jillian took my hand and squeezed it.

"Thank you, Zachary."

The waiter returned with our drink orders. A glass of Merlot for Jillian and—you guessed it—

a glass of soda for me. As for dinner, Jason and Arlen both ordered steaks. I guess when one lived in Alaska, and there was crab aplenty, the appeal of freshly caught crustacean wasn't that strong. Marianne ordered a salmon dish, while Shannon selected a surf and turf option. As for me, I didn't need to decide on anything. I was here for some authentic Alaskan snow crab. It might be pricey, but it was nowhere near the price we had to pay for a crab dinner when we visited Juneau on our previous visit to the state. And, I already knew Jillian was going to order the same thing.

Once the waitress left, I pulled out my phone and gave everyone a grin.

"Thanks for coming, guys. By now, most of you will have heard of Sherlock and Watson. They're the reason why we're all here. Jillian and I have this tradition back home where, if we're working on a case, we'll gather all our friends together and try to figure out what the dogs are trying to tell us."

"Seriously?" Arlen asked, growing interested.

"It's how they work," Jillian tried to explain.

"No, I mean, your dogs—they're Sherlock and Watson? The famous detective dogs that went to England?"

I nodded. "The one and the same."

Arlen sat up straight in her chair and set her drink on the table.

"Wait just a minute. That footage I saw from YouTube … that was the real Queen of England petting your two dogs?"

"The one and the same," I said, growing wistful. "She even attended our wedding. I was truly sorry to hear of her passing. I'm so very honored we had a chance to meet her in person."

"What you said before was true?" Jason demanded. "About your dogs. That means you *are* working a case! It's why you're here, isn't it? Listen, you gotta let me help! It's the least I can do. Whadya say?"

"What do you say?" Jillian corrected.

"What do you say?" Arlen echoed.

The two women looked at each other and laughed.

"Just what I need," Jason grumped. "Two women correctin' my grammar."

I looked at Marianne.

"We haven't told them anything. But, this would probably go a whole lot smoother if you'd be willing to tell them a few details. Jason, you *are* helping. You all are."

Marianne nodded, and then sighed. She faced Jason and Arlen.

"A penguin chick was stolen from us several days ago."

Arlen gasped and her hand flew to her face.

"No. Not a chick! How old?"

"Just a few days," Shannon added. "And if we don't get it back in less than two days, then our facility is never going to gain the accreditation it needs to operate, and we will be forced to close."

Arlen took Jason's hand and clenched it tightly.

"How can we help?"

I waggled my cell phone in front of everyone.

"Help us figure out what all of this means, and how it could possibly pertain to this case. Now, we all know what this is, right? It's a smart phone. I routinely take pictures of whatever catches the dogs' attention, with the sole intent of studying them at a later date. What I need all of you to do is look at the pictures and see if there's some type of common denominator. Somehow, what we'll be looking at will lead us to the person—or persons—responsible for this theft."

"Let's see them," Marianne said.

"All right, here we go. First picture was taken on our first day here. Shannon, remember the mother moose and her baby?"

"The one in the middle of the road," Dr. Rozhkov's assistant recalled.

"Exactly. Well, that was the first time Sherlock and Watson fixated on something. They both sat, which meant it was time to snap a picture. Go ahead and pass that around, will you?"

"It's just a moose," Jason said, when my phone found its way into his hands. "A cow and her calf. Nothing spectacular there, I'm afraid."

"Wait for it," I told him, holding up a finger. "Now, the next picture is … the same thing. Right. Okay, moving on. Next up is something we found when I took the dogs out to go potty, by our cabin."

Shannon being immediately on my left, took my phone and studied the image.

"What is it? Some type of sculpture?"

"It's a dragon," I said. "See how the wings are partly extended, and the tail is wrapped around the body? It's hard to tell at first, seeing how it's made of scrap metal."

Jason scratched his beard. "I don't get it. How do you know you're supposed to be looking at a dragon? Maybe your dogs were looking at metal? Or junk?"

"Remember the toy from your boat?"

Jason's eyes widened with shock.

"Holy cow. I forgot about that."

"What toy from your boat?" Arlen asked.

I held up a finger. "We're coming to that."

Jason frowned. "How is a moose and a dragon supposed to be connected?"

Arlen rolled her eyes and used her own hand, still intwined with his, to thump him on his chest.

"That's the whole point. Somehow, they *are* related. It's up to us to figure out how."

"How long?" Jason asked.

"How long *what*?" I wanted to know.

"How long does it usually take you to figure out what you're looking at?"

I shrugged. "It usually doesn't make sense until the case has been solved. Logic would suggest that at some point, we should be able to figure out what we're looking at, but noooooo."

Jason and Arlen both laughed.

"A moose family and a dragon sculpture," Marianne said, sighing. "I'm afraid I don't see the connection, either."

My phone was passed around the table. No one, I'm sorry to say, had anything to add.

"All right, we're moving on," I said, swiping to the next picture. "Right, here we have … another moose reference. This time, we have a moose crossing sign. By the time I was able to take a picture, we had already passed it."

"That's why we're looking at the backside of a sign?" Shannon asked. "Was this when you were with me?"

"Right. I think this happened on our second trip to CCCP."

"And there's no chance the sign had a picture of a different animal?" Jason wanted to know.

I shook my head. "Nope. You know the kind. Black picture of a moose, on a yield-shaped sign."

"I can't wait to hear how a moose could have anything to do with a penguin robbery," Jason said.

"You and me both," I chuckled. "Everyone have a look? Good. Now, who's got my phone? There it is. Thanks. Okay, next up, we have … hmm. I forgot about this one. Marianne, you'll have to confirm this for me, but I think this one is a picture of CCCP's main computer control station?"

Dr. Rozhkov needed only a brief moment to confirm that it was.

"When was this?" the facility's CEO asked. "The first day?"

I looked at Jillian, who nodded.

"Yes. Sherlock and Watson plunked their furry

butts in front of the desk and refused to move."

Jason snickered.

"A moose, dragon, and a computer," Shannon mused. "I think this is making it worse, not better."

Jillian laughed. "I agree."

Jason looked at the photo, shrugged, and passed it to his wife. Arlen, I'm very pleased to say, gasped with surprise and looked up.

"I see why you took the picture!"

Our table fell deathly silent.

"I'm all ears," I said, leaning forward anxiously.

"Me, too. Babe, whatcha got?"

"What do you have?" Jillian corrected, with a smile.

"What do you have?" Arlen echoed. "And look. Look at the computer's display."

I took my phone back and studied it. There were at least thirty icons on the desktop, some for folder shortcuts, others for programs. I wasn't sure if there was one I was supposed to be looking at, but before I could ask, Jillian suddenly leaned close and gasped.

"Oh, my! I never noticed that, either."

Cursing silently, I held my phone close to my face. That's when I noticed the display, or rather, the *desktop wallpaper*. It was a fantasy scene, and sure enough, there was a clearly visible creature in the background. It was actually more of a silhouette, but unmistakably a dragon.

"The computer has dragon-themed wallpaper," I reported.

Marianne's eyes widened. She held out her hand, wanting to see the image. Once I passed it over, she was silent as she studied the image.

"Can you see it?" I asked.

"Oh, I see it," Marianne confirmed. "I'm just trying to remember if that picture has always been there. Shannon, what do you say? Can you remember if a dragon has always been on the main computer?"

The assistant's brow furrowed. "I think so. I can't think of a time when I didn't see this particular picture."

Jason took back the phone and zoomed in on the display.

"I'll be damned. Didn't see that coming. I always told you that you've got good eyes, babe."

Arlen blushed, but smiled gratefully at her husband.

"More dragons," I said, as I reclaimed my phone. "Moving on. Okay, this ought to be interesting. Next up, we have a picture of the Lotus Blossom Apothecary. I remember this one, too. We were walking by all those shops, and the dogs decided to stop, and I have no idea why. Anyone?"

"The apothecary," Marianne said, thinking. "It's just a pharmacy. I get my prescriptions filled there."

Shannon held up a hand. "So do I."

"Is there anything remarkable about that shop?" Jillian asked. "Does anything stand out?"

Marianne shrugged. "Not really. They have

everything you'd expect to find in a drug store, and then some. First aid supplies, cough medicines, pain killers, and so on."

"What was there before it was a drug store?" I asked. "Maybe it's relevant?"

My wife smiled. "Ooooo, good one, Zachary. Let's see if I can find anything out online."

"It's been a drug store as long as I can remember," Jason said. "Been in it a few times, mostly for your standard, over-the-counter meds."

"Apparently, that apothecary has been around since the turn of the century," Jillian reported. "It says it's changed owners a few times, but it always stayed in the family."

"Moose, dragons, and drugs," I recalled, ticking off my fingers as I did. "Before anyone asks, I haven't a clue what it means."

"Well, I guess moose makes sense," Arlen began. "After all, this *is* Alaska."

"Tell them what you've done so far to validate the moose clue," Jillian urged.

I snapped my fingers. "That's right. Not that long ago, we tried to figure out if *moose* could be the name of a person. As it happens, we were provided a local phone book, only after multiple attempts at locating someone by that name, nothing was found."

"How about a business name?" Marianne asked.

I gave our small group a recap of our attempts at confirming our theory Moose Pharmaceuticals was connected.

"I was so certain we had finally found a clue," Jillian said, with a sigh.

"You and me both," I agreed. "But, like everything else, it turned up a dead end. Ready for the next? Here we go. Hmm. Forgot about this one, too." I turned to Jason. "This one was because of you."

"The toy dragon," Jason guessed.

"No. The banana."

"Are you sure it wasn't just the food talking?" Shannon asked. "I know dogs love bananas."

"I mentioned that, too," Jason added.

"It was considered," I admitted, "but just as quickly disregarded. Why? Sherlock and Watson both sat, and refused to touch the banana until I took a picture. Once I did, they couldn't get to it fast enough."

The table fell silent.

"I want to know about this toy," Shannon told me.

"That makes two of us," Arlen said.

Jason turned to his wife. "Remember when we gave your brother and his family a ride on *DeeDee*? They had Matthew with them. I didn't know he brought his toys on board. Well, one was left behind, and somehow became wedged into a panel. Their dogs found it and stared at it, as though it was made of sausage. I didn't think anything of it, yet those two," and he pointed at us, "thought it was the Holy Grail. But, I will admit, I see why they acted that way."

"Dragons," Marianne softly repeated. She closed her eyes and sat back in her chair. "How could dragons possibly be involved here? Unless ... what if these references are nothing more than a request to pay attention to the one thing that actually *has* made sense?"

"What's that?" Shannon asked.

"The picture of the main computer. That one computer controls everything. What if your two dogs are trying to tell us to take a closer look at our master computer?"

"What does it do?" I asked.

Marianne sat back in her chair and let out a heavy sigh.

"What *can't* it do? It's what we use to track and monitor each of our birds. It holds the brains of our security system: door locks, access points, our database files, medical history for the birds, incubation logs, and the list goes on and on. I'm starting to think I need to take a closer look at that computer."

"Would you know what you're looking for?" Shannon asked her boss.

"Honestly? No. But, I have to try."

"Don't you have an IT guy?" I asked. "He'd be the one to run a diagnostic check on it, wouldn't you think?"

"Zachary, what if *he* is the one who tampered with it?" Jillian asked.

Marianne looked thoughtful. "Chris Emery may be young, but I wouldn't put it past him to ... no!

I will *not* start second-guessing my people. I trust Chris. He's a good kid. No, whatever happened, *if* something happened, was done by someone other than one of us."

Jason tapped the table to get my attention. He pointed at my phone, which was next to my soda glass.

"Is that the last of the pictures?"

"Oh. Let's see. After Jason's banana, we have ..."

Jillian, Arlen, and Shannon all giggled.

"... we have some pictures of otters. Oh, this is the wildlife tour. Otter pic, otter pic, whew, a whole lotta otter pics. And now we have the eagle pics. I'm surprised I have any room left on my phone. And now it's the whales. Although, in my defense, that was incredibly cool. I've never been that close to whales before. Hey, here we go. This was on Ainsworth Island, at their lodge. A moose family appeared, and wouldn't you know it? The corgis both sat and remained motionless the entire time."

"Another moose clue," Jason moaned. "It's rugged country out here. There's bound to be wildlife. It probably doesn't mean anything."

"Dragon toy," I reminded my new friend, without looking up from my phone. "And this makes the third time they've focused on a moose."

"Yeah, yeah."

Arlen thumped him in the stomach.

"Okay, I just found the last picture," I announced. "It's hard to see, but you can tell there's a plane up there, in the sky."

"One of the float planes?" Jason asked.

"Float planes?" I repeated. "Guess I've been calling them wrong all this time. All right, see the float plane? I couldn't tell if Sherlock and Watson were watching the plane or not. They were already on the ground."

"Were both watching?" Jillian wanted to know.

"Both of 'em," I confirmed.

"Hmm. At that distance, you can't really tell anything about it," Jillian said.

I placed my phone back into my pocket after it had made the rounds.

"That's all of them. I'll now open the floor for suggestions."

It was suddenly so quiet you could've heard a pin drop.

"Don't everyone start talking at once," I chuckled.

"Moose Pharmaceuticals," Jillian said. "I'm thinking they have something to do with it."

"The owner is deceased," I reminded her. "And we can't find any surviving family."

"Moose Pharmaceuticals? It's too convenient," my wife insisted. "There must be a connection."

Marianne's phone started ringing just then. She looked at the display, excused herself, and headed toward the door. I was about ready to suggest we call Chris, CCCP's computer guy, to work some of his magic and see if he could find anything out about the family when I saw Marianne hurrying back to the table. Her face was ashen, and she appeared to be sputtering.

"Is everything all right?" I quietly asked. When she didn't respond, I rose to my feet and guided her to her chair. "Doc? Marianne? Deep breaths. Collect your thoughts."

Dr. Rozhkov reached for her water and took several large gulps. A few moments later, a look of firm resolve appeared on her face. She shoved her phone into her purse and whipped her coat off the back of her chair.

"We need to get back to CCCP," Marianne told us.

"What's wrong?" Jillian asked, growing alarmed. "What's happened?"

"That was Katia. There's been a break-in!"

EIGHT

"I know you've already explained what's happened, Katia," Marianne said. "However, everyone is now here. I just need you to go through it all once more. What were you doing here? What prompted you to come back?"

I glanced at my watch and saw that it was nearly seven p.m.

"Just a moment. Do you have a swing keeper, or someone that's monitoring the facility whenever you guys aren't here?"

Marianne pointed at the master computer.

"That's why we sank so much into this system. Everything can be run from this control room. Everything is automated, and it can be accessed remotely, but only by someone with admin privileges. At CCCP, that's me or Chris. As for the system, it'll arm itself once the last person leaves for the day."

"And when is that?" Jillian wanted to know.

I figured I should be taking notes, so I retrieved my notebook.

"Five p.m.," Dr. Rozhkov answered.

"When did you get here?" Shannon asked.

"Ten minutes ago," Katia answered, in her Russian accent.

I pointed at the computer.

"Then, why didn't that thing warn you guys that someone was here after hours?"

"That's what I don't understand," Marianne said, exasperated. "It should have, and it didn't. It's highly concerning."

Shannon raised a hand. "I'm sorry, but what prompted you to come back, Katia?"

The animal keeper held up a folded purple *something*.

"What's that?" I asked.

"My hat. It's favorite. Mistake. I left it here."

I noticed Jillian was slowing scanning the room. She then turned to study the hallway leading back to the foyer. Finally, she turned to Katia and raised a hand.

"Katia, I'm sorry, but I have to ask. How did you know there had been a robbery here? Everything looks the same to me."

A second bundle of clothes was produced.

"I found inside, near door. The pegs … for coats? It was hanging there."

"What is it?" I asked. "A coat?"

"Looks like a scarf," Marianne said. "And you're sure this doesn't belong to anyone here?"

"I am last. Nothing was there. Then, come inside. Something there."

"I have another question."

We all turned to my wife.

"The system is supposed to be armed. Does the simple act of stepping inside disarm it? I wouldn't think it'd be much of a security system if it did."

Dr. Rozhkov shook her head. "No. To arm it? Yes. Once we all leave, the computer senses we've left, and it'll protect itself, regardless of the time. But, to disarm it? No. There's a keypad just inside the door, on the left. The proper code must be entered."

"Or what?" Jillian asked. "Who gets notified first? You or the police?"

"Like any alarm system, it should be the police first," Marianne said.

My wife looked at the Russian animal keeper and offered her a smile.

"Katia, do you remember if you punched in the code to turn *off* the system?"

The keeper's eyes widened with surprise.

"I … no. I come in. I see hanging scarf. I know someone here. I don't know who."

"Then what?" I wanted to know. "You suspected someone was here. What did you find that convinced you a robbery had taken place?"

"Green book gone."

Dr. Rozhkov's head jerked up.

"The log? You're kidding. Are you sure?"

"I was last to use. Enter times I turn eggs. I leave. Once I see scarf, I hurry to eggs. See book gone."

"Omigod, the eggs!" Marianne cried.

We all hurried down the stairs, with the good

doctor taking nearly two at a time near the end. By the time we caught up with her, she was at the incubator, staring through the glass walls at the rows of penguin eggs. Dr. Rozhkov was dabbing at her eyes with a tissue.

"Tell me they didn't," Jillian began, as a look of horror appeared on her face.

"They didn't. I'm so relieved."

"What is this book you're talking about?" I asked. "Some type of log book?"

"It's essentially a diary of what our keepers have done in order to achieve a viable egg," Marianne said, using a quiet tone. "Incubation times, temps, humidity, light level, and so on. It's our guide in order to be able to replicate what we've done."

I held my hands up in a time-out gesture.

"Whoa. Are you telling me if someone got their hands on that book, they'd be able to replicate your success?"

Marianne groaned. "Yes."

"Does anyone else think that whoever pulled this off was sincerely hoping that no one would be coming back this evening?" I asked.

"Looks that way to me," Shannon answered.

"Whoever took it was planning on copying it," Jillian guessed. "The plan was probably to return the book later tonight, without anyone knowing a copy had been made."

Marianne turned to Katia and threw her arms around her, encompassing her in a hug.

"I appreciate your forgetfulness. But now, we

must recover our log book."

Katia nodded. "Agreed."

A thought occurred, and it had me frowning.

"Doc? How much do you know about your security system here?"

Marianne shrugged. "Enough, I suppose. Why do you ask?"

"Can you tell if the system has been tampered with? I'm starting to wonder if your computer system is the source of the dragon clues. I think the dogs were telling us to pay attention to the dragon. The dragon that lives *here*."

Dr. Rozhkov scowled. "That's disturbing on so many levels, but I understand where you're coming from. Back upstairs. Let's see what we can figure out."

We all returned to the control room and crowded around the main terminal. Marianne pulled the chair away from the console and sat down. She entered a few commands and waited for the program's interface to open. When it didn't, she tried again. After a few moments, it became clear that there was, indeed, something wrong with the facility's main computer.

Marianne groaned and tried again.

I nudged Shannon's shoulder.

"Any chance I could get you to run me to the cabin? I think we need a set of canine eyes on this."

"Of course."

"Jillian, will you be okay here? I'm gonna go get the dogs."

"Of course. Hurry back."

Twenty minutes later, Sherlock and Watson *strutted* into the room, with me holding their leashes. I swear those two were enjoying the attention they were receiving, because if I didn't know any better, I'd say they were taking their time making their way over to the others.

"I'm glad your Royal Canineships could tear yourselves away from your busy schedule to help us," I sniggered.

Sherlock gave me the stink-eye. He glanced once at Watson and started to head for the closest person when he paused. Sniffing the air, the feisty corgi turned to look up at the giant wall screen, which was currently displaying the computer's desktop image, namely the fantasy dragon picture. A few seconds later, Watson did the same. Then, both corgis sat.

"They're staring at the computer again," Jillian reported. "I'm assuming that could only mean there's something wrong with it?"

"Confirmed," Marianne said. "I can't get the program to open. What the heck is going on around here?"

"Can you reboot it?" I asked. "Maybe, as with any computer, it just needs to be turned off, and then back on."

Marianne's fingers danced across the keyboard. Then, a prompt appeared, warning the computer had received a request to restart. Dr. Rozhkov confirmed it and down it went, with the monitor turning into a solid black wall.

I guess I'm too used to my own personal computer shutting down, but I could power it down and then back up in less than fifteen seconds. This beast took nearly ten minutes. I know. I timed it. When it finally returned to the desktop, and the icons appeared, Marianne tried once more to activate the security program.

A prompt for credentials appeared. Dr. Rozhkov sighed with relief and logged in. The screen went blank, hesitated for a few moments, and then displayed all the feeds from the various cameras.

"Thank heavens. We're up and running. Oh, that could have ended so badly."

"What was taken?" I asked. The room fell silent. "Doc, didn't you say that CCCP had been robbed again? What was taken?"

We all turned to Katia.

"You said it was a robbery, and not a break-in."

"My English, no very good," Katia admitted. "Robbery, break-in. I thought mean same thing."

"Not quite," Marianne said, smiling. Her smile melted into a frown when she saw me.

For the record, I was looking at Sherlock and Watson. Both had perked up and were looking around the room, as though they expected the boogeyman to jump out at them at any moment. If I didn't know any better, I'd say they were acting like ...

"*Woof.*"

It was low, fairly quiet, but loud enough to

silence everyone in the room. I could tell people were looking at Sherlock as though they had never heard such a soft bark before. Then again, I'm not sure they have ever met a dog as intelligent as him. Was Sherlock trying to tell us something?

"Awwooowooo," Sherlock argued, making his howl low and guttural.

Now he's a mind reader?

"What is it, boy?" I quietly asked.

That's when I saw something that made my blood run cold. The hairs on Sherlock's back were standing up. That only happened if …

"He's still here," I whispered.

Jillian's eyes widened. Marianne stifled a curse and reached for her desk phone. Frowning, she replaced the receiver.

"No dial tone. Someone has locked us out."

"Video still works," I reminded her. "The phones don't? Even after the computer has been restarted?"

"I'd say someone wants to make sure we can't raise the alarm," Jillian said.

"I say we split up and find this bastard," I suggested.

"No splitting up," the head of CCCP ordered.

"No way, Zachary," Jillian said, at the same time. "It's too risky. Whoever is here could be armed."

"Precisely," Marianne said. "We stick together. I guess we stay here and wait for him to show up on the video feeds?"

"That's not going to work," Jillian said.

"Why not?" Shannon asked.

My wife pointed at the big bank of video feeds.

"We're all looking at a recording. Look, there we are from earlier today."

"Can someone call the police?" Marianne asked. "I don't seem to have a signal in here."

"Same here," I said, as I checked my phone. "I know it was working earlier. That doesn't bode well."

"They're jamming our signal," Jillian observed. "We have underestimated these people. What should we do now?"

I pointed at the dogs.

"Let them do their work. I say we find this guy. Maybe we can check to see if there's anything else missing? It might let us know what they're up to."

Jillian looked at Dr. Rozhkov.

"Marianne, what do you think?"

"We stick together," she decided. "There's safety in numbers. Mr. Anderson, we're in your hands."

I nodded. "Roger that. Sherlock. Watson. It's time we figured out what's going on here. Show us what we need to see, okay?"

My two corgis took their time giving themselves a good shaking before heading off. From the looks of things, our first stop was going to be the basement. Once we all arrived on the medical floor, the dogs wasted no time in heading toward the incubator.

"No, not there," I heard Marianne plead, from behind me.

Both corgis veered and, instead, sniffed along the row of fridges and freezers lining the wall. Sherlock appeared to choose one at random, sniffed along the bottom, and then sat. Watson finished her own inspection and chose that unit to stop at, too. Together, they turned to look at our small group.

"What's in there?" I asked.

Marianne turned to Katia, who nodded. She smiled at the dogs, shooed them out of the way so they wouldn't get hit by the opening doors, and studied the contents.

"Is freezer. Fish. Frozen fish. Smelt, herring, krill. Is food we feed penguins."

As one, everyone turned to look at me. I, in turn, glanced down at my two dogs. Sherlock and Watson were still sitting, but now they both had looks of exasperation on their faces, as though they couldn't believe I hadn't figured out what they wanted us to figure out.

Wait. Fish?

"Using what's in this freezer," I began, "can you feed a baby penguin?"

"Infant penguins typically eat regurgitated fish," Marianne explained. "While we obviously can't provide that for the chick, we *can* make a type of paste from ground smelt and krill. Put that in … oh, dear lord. I see where you're going with this. With the log book, and the fish, they could … Katia, I need a quick inventory of this freezer. We need to know if anything is missing."

"Da. You? Can help?"

I passed the leashes to Jillian.

"Absolutely. Pass me those gloves."

It took nearly thirty minutes, but we had our answer. Unfortunately, it wasn't good. One box each of smelt and krill was missing. Each box weighed nearly thirty pounds frozen, so that meant whoever had the chick now had enough fish to feed it for probably a week or two. Add in the missing book, and they now had the instructions to go along with it.

"I have to report this," Marianne sadly stated. "We're down one box each of smelt and krill. This will be the end of us. I'm sorry. I have no other option."

I held up a hand. "Wait. We're not there yet."

"Yes, we are," Dr. Rozhkov argued. "What more can we do?"

"Don't you get it?" I returned. "The chick. It's still alive. And, it's clearly not somewhere in the facility. No, it's somewhere else, and if the perp is coming here to steal fish ..."

"It's somewhere nearby!" Jillian exclaimed. "Marianne, Zachary is right. We can't give up now!"

"What more can we do?" Dr. Rozhkov groaned.

I pointed at the freezer. "Is that all that was taken? Some frozen fish? I think we need to look for anything else that's missing. It might tell us more about who might've taken the chick, and most importantly, where the chick is being held."

"Of course. If you'll excuse me, I'll go call

everyone in. This is going to take all of us."

Nearly two hours later, we all reconvened in the control room. All the animal keepers were there, along with the veterinarian, Chris from IT, us, Dr. Rozhkov, Shannon, and a fair number of significant others. No one could tell if anything else had been taken.

Sherlock and Watson were reclining on the floor, near my feet. Jillian and I had taken seats next to Marianne, and together, the three of us were silent, lost in our thoughts. I heard Sherlock roll onto his side, and when I looked, I suddenly had a strong suspicion I knew what else had been stolen.

"You have heating blankets here?" I asked, breaking the silence.

Marianne looked at the keepers. Penny, Siggie, and Katia all nodded in unison.

"Could someone check?" I asked. "I think you'll find one of them is missing."

Heads turned until everyone was staring at me, dogs included. Penny shrugged, and hurried off. Several minutes later, she was back, and from the sound of her wheezing, she had sprinted all the way here.

"One's missing!"

"How did you know that?" Marianne demanded.

"This is starting to make sense," I said, ignoring (for now) the CEO's question. "Check your meds, vitamins, and I'm really sorry to say this, but check your transport crates. Also, I could be wrong here, but you might want to check to see if you're missing some paperwork. Specifically, a form that authorizes the transport of a protected species."

Jillian's eyes lit up. "They're planning on shipping the chick out of town. Oh, no!"

"You heard him," Dr. Rozhkov snapped. "Check to see if he's right. I need to know if they're planning on moving the chick."

It only took ten minutes to confirm I was right on the money. Chris, responsible for the facility's IT systems, sidled close.

"Dude, I gotta ask you something. How'd you know what this guy is planning on doing?"

"It fits," I answered. "I'm guessing whoever stole the chick has a buyer lined up, and now needs to guarantee delivery of a healthy penguin, otherwise, what's the point?"

"What's wrong with your dogs?" Chris suddenly asked.

"Hmm?" I heard a whine and started looking for Sherlock and Watson. I found them near the main doors leading out, toward the outer yards. The sun had long set, and if not for a couple of nearby light posts, it'd be pitch black. Anticipating the rapidly dropping temps, I shivered. Did the dogs need to go outside? After all, when was the last time I took them on a potty break?

The whines switched to snarls. Coming from corgis, that was saying something. Shocked, I turned to look at my dogs when I noticed both were on their feet and both had their hackles raised. Something had spooked them, and from the direction they were facing, it was coming from the kitchen. That was when we heard it.

The front door slammed closed.

"Where is everyone?" I asked, raising my voice. "Who just headed outside?"

Dr. Rozhkov appeared. "No one has gone anywhere, why?"

"The front door just closed."

"Impossible. We're all accounted for."

Jillian gasped and took my hand.

"It must be the person who broke in, Zachary! You were right! They were still in the building!"

Shannon hurried by us, holding her keys.

"Don't just stand there, come on! We can't lose them!"

The corgis started barking as though a poodle had just sauntered by and stolen their favorite toy. Both dogs switched to their alternate identities, that of Clydesdales, and pulled my sorry butt toward the foyer, whether I was willing or not.

"Stay here," I ordered, as I hastily pulled on my coat. "I'll keep you posted."

Jillian nodded. "Please do. Shannon, don't do anything I wouldn't do."

Shannon nodded. "You got it."

Once we were back in the van, and Shannon had spun the tires in an attempt to get the bulky vehicle in motion as soon as possible, she pointed the vehicle east and stomped on the accelerator.

I felt, rather than saw, the van slip and slide on

the road. There, visible in the distance as nothing more than a speck of light color against the dark green trees of the surrounding forest, was the vehicle we were pursuing. I saw a brief flash of red and realized our thief must've hit the brakes. I also realized we were rapidly gaining on them.

"Whoa! Maybe we should slow down?"

"There shouldn't be any black ice on the road," Shannon reported, as she guided the van toward the small stretch of Lincoln Street, which constituted the entirety of Sitka's downtown district. "Granted, it's cold, but I do believe it was warm enough earlier to keep the roads dry. At least, that's my hope."

I studied the car as we neared it. It was at least a half-mile away when we first saw it. Now, it was no more than a quarter-mile away. Rusty wheels started turning as I realized why.

"He's driving something not suitable for these conditions. What idiot, in their right minds, would come to Alaska and *not* have a suitable car?"

"I can't tell what it is," Shannon said. "Can you?"

I squinted at the road. I couldn't quite make out what type of vehicle it was, but there was something about the shape of the tail lights. I *know* I've seen those before. I just had to remember where.

"Wait, something's happened," Shannon said, frowning. "That car is accelerating, and it's moving fast. I think we're ... Sherlock! Watson! Could I get you guys to stop barking?"

Both of my dogs hadn't shut up since we had heard the front door slam. I know most people wouldn't think of corgis as being vicious dogs, but if you were to hear them, then you'd probably wonder how such nasty barks could come from such cute fluffballs. However, once you see them, you'd know the only body part you'd have to be concerned about would be your ankles.

The red tail lights vanished in the distance. Cursing silently, I gave each of my dogs a friendly scratch. When they looked my way, I pointed out the windshield.

"You've done it before, guys. I need you to do it again. Find that car, would you?"

Sherlock gave my hand a friendly lick and promptly looked right, just as we approached one of the few intersections in town.

"Turn here," I ordered. "Right."

Tiny, powdery flakes began falling. Without missing a beat, Shannon adjusted the controls and slipped the van into off-roading mode.

"Figures. Looks like it's started snowing again."

"I noticed," I groaned. "Seriously, Sitka isn't that big. If you don't slow down, then *you* are the one who's gonna have to 'splain yourself to my wife."

Shannon laughed and guided the van farther away from the town center. Oncoming traffic tapered off, and before we knew it, we were seemingly the only ones on the road.

"Are we going the right way?"

I looked at the dogs. Both corgis, I might add,

were on their feet and facing forward.

"It would seem so. Just ... wait a moment! I think we passed the road we need. They're looking left, and now they've turned to look behind us."

"We did pass a road back there," Shannon reported. "Hang on, there's not much room to turn around. There we go. Now, it should be just around the bend. See it? Do they want us to turn?"

Sherlock and Watson were now looking right, which is the direction the road took from the other direction.

"That's affirmative."

The van turned onto Shotgun Street. The road narrowed considerably, where I think we'd be in trouble if we happened across another car. In this case, I don't think either of us were too concerned about traffic. What *did* catch our eye was the large tree currently blocking the road. Ordinarily, I would have thought that the amount of snow in its branches would be the reason why it toppled, but something about the sudden appearance of our roadblock had me telling the dogs to stay put. Stepping outside, I hurried over to the trunk for a closer look.

It wasn't an accident. The tree had very discernible cuts, made from a chainsaw. This was done on purpose. Someone had helped our thief escape!

Shannon's cell rang. She tapped the display and allowed the van's electronics to answer the phone.

"Tell me you got him," Dr. Rozhkov pleaded.

"Tell me you have something I can give the police."

"We lost him," Shannon sadly reported. "We pursued him down to Lincoln, and then out to Sawmill Creek Road. We followed him east, until we hit this tiny road, Shotgun, and found that the road was blocked."

The call fell silent as this news was relayed to others in the room.

"Blocked by what?" I heard someone ask. One of the keepers?

"A tree," I said, chiming in.

"It's snowing here," Marianne informed us. "It's probably just ..."

"... taken down by a chainsaw?" I casually asked, interrupting her before she could attribute the fallen tree to natural causes.

"Someone cut it down?" I heard my wife ask.

"On purpose," I confirmed. "All to keep us from following. Did you guys find anything else out on your end?"

"There was nothing else missing," Marianne confirmed, "and I'm very sorry to say, no trace of the missing log book. This confirms it. We have to report this."

"This is a small town," I argued. "There are only so many people here. From the sounds of it, this guy is still in the area, but not for much longer. We need to notify someone, all right, but not who you think. It's time, don't you think? It's time to contact the press, or police, or the general public. We need to release what we know and ask the public to become our ears and eyes."

"We don't know what he looks like," Jillian protested.

"But, we do know what he was driving," I said. "We at least saw that much."

"I didn't see anything," Shannon quietly told me. "How did you?"

"I just remembered where I've seen those tail lights before. Three vertical stripes, on either side of the car. I know of only one type of car that fits that description. Our thief is driving a Mustang."

NINE

Y ou're looking for a muscle car," I instructed early the following morning, holding my cell out in front of me. "A Ford Mustang. I recognized the tail lights. What's that? Year? I don't know. Umm, fairly new. Late model, I guess. Color? It was dark. Dark blue, or black, or maybe gray. Yes, I'm certain of it."

"Who's he talking to?" Shannon asked, as she and Chris joined us in front of the main computer in the Control Room.

"Someone from the local police department," Jillian reported. "A detective, I think."

"You think it's a Mustang?" Chris asked, rather loudly. I could hear the skepticism in his voice.

I'm not very proud of myself for what I did next, but I turned to this younger kid and pointed at my cell at the same time I gave him a disapproving frown.

"It's just not something you'd find here, in Sitka," Chris protested. "It's not a practical car for driving around our town. That's all I'm saying. Especially at this time of year."

"Hush," Jillian scolded.

"He's got a point," I quietly mouthed. "No, I'm here, sorry. What's that? No, I don't have anything … wait. Let me think. I'm sure there was something else. Oh! I've got it! Wow. Score one for the memory banks. Look, as that Mustang put some distance between the two of us, I heard a very distinctive roar in the engine. That car sounded as though it had been modified, like someone had installed a supercharger. No, I'm not a mechanic, nor am I even a car aficionado. I researched the topic a few years back for a book I was writing. No, it wasn't any type of technical manual. I'm a novelist. What kind? Hoo, boy. I was afraid you were going to ask that. I'm a romance novelist. Mm-hmm, you heard that right. And now you're laughing. Well, Detective Taneidí, I could respond to that, and I'm fighting every urge to do just that, but I promised my wife I'd try to be nicer on the phone. For now, I'll just say that I know a little about cars."

"A supercharged Mustang?" Chris repeated, having overheard my tip. "In Sitka? I doubt it."

"You're welcome, detective," I was saying, as I listened to the police officer thank me for my time. "If we find anything out here, we'll be sure to let you know."

"What'd he say?" Jillian asked.

"He doubted my observations about the car," I said, shrugging, "but I was clear enough to pique his interest. He's going to see if anyone in town happens to own a late-model, dark Mustang. If so, he said he'll see if he can determine its location during the last twenty-four hours."

"I called my contact at the police department," Marianne announced, as she descended from the second floor. "They've instituted a full lock-down of the town. Since there aren't any roads that take you out of here, the piers are under orders to prevent anyone from departing, and all planes have been grounded. I'm also told you spoke with the detective? Captain Pharell said he's Tlingit, and probably the smartest person he knows."

"Tlingit?" I repeated. "He's Inuit?"

Dr. Rozhkov nodded. "Yes."

"I got the impression he thinks I'm as high as a kite," I said, sighing. "And do you know what? I can't say I blame him. I mean, I'm an outsider, spinning one hell of a yarn about yellow planes, a herd of moose, and an apothecary shop."

"Dragons," Jillian reminded me. "Don't forget about the dragons."

I snapped my fingers. "Right. Let's face it. I wouldn't believe me, either."

Jillian held out a hand.

"Come on, Zachary. Let's go for a walk."

"Who willingly walks outside when it's snowing?" I asked, bewildered.

"Not outside, you silly man. Marianne, is Dr. Tanko currently here?"

Dr. Rozhkov checked her watch. "He told me he finished his last batch of wellness checks, so I believe he headed home."

"Let's go downstairs," Jillian suggested.

With each of us holding a leash, we headed down to the floor dedicated to veterinary medicine. As with most doctor offices, there was a small area just past the stairwell, which served as a sitting room for those waiting to speak with the Nigerian doctor. Jillian headed to the closest chair and sat down.

"Something's bothering you. Can you tell me what it is?"

I took the next seat.

"I have to admit, I'm starting to have my doubts."

"About what?" my wife wanted to know.

I pointed at the floor.

"This place. This case. Let's face it. We're several days in, and we're no closer to figuring out what happened to that poor chick than the first day we were here. Don't get me wrong. The corgis are doing their thing. It's just that … I don't feel like I'm doing, well, *my* thing. We've looked at a wide variety of clues, but thus far, we haven't been able to determine who—or what—we should be focusing our attention on. By this time in the case, we typically have an idea who's at fault, or who's the person of interest. It's when we call in the cavalry and let Vance show up, point his gun, and deal with the bad guys."

Jillian was silent as she let me ramble.

"What?" I asked, as I took Jillian's hands in my own. "Say something, would you?"

"You're starting to lose hope, aren't you?"

"Well, wouldn't you?" I countered. "You've got to admit, the dogs have an unbroken track record at this point. It stands to reason, sooner or later, that record is going to fall. Well, I think we can consider the winning streak broken. We're nowhere close to solving this mystery."

"A solution will present itself," Jillian assured me. "It always does. Someone, somewhere, will be able to figure this out."

"And what if they don't? I mean, that should be me. What if *I* don't?"

My wife held up her hands.

"Give it some time. This case isn't over. Sherlock and Watson will come through. They always do."

"Do you have any theories?" I asked.

Jillian shrugged. "Only that whoever took the chick in the first place is still in town, and looking for a way to smuggle it *out.*"

I shrugged. "In town, out of town, who freakin' knows?"

My wife gave my hands a squeeze and a firm shake.

"Hey, don't you even think about doubting yourself now. You and your dogs have been doing this long enough now to know whether or not you're on the right track. Have the answers presented themselves yet? Obviously not. Has there ever been a case where the dogs couldn't solve it? No. You just have to be patient."

"We're running out of time," I reminded her. "The guy who hands out the accreditations is due here in less than two days, and we're still one penguin short."

Sherlock looked up and met our eyes. He snuggled next to my leg and whined. Naturally, Watson was on her feet in record time, and approached from the opposite side. Together, the two of them leaned into my leg as they each circled around, like wagon trains in an old western movie trying to protect itself from outside attackers.

"It's okay, guys," I told the corgis. "I'm just having a hard time trying to figure out what you're telling us. If you'd like to throw me a hint every so often, now would be a great time to do it."

Sherlock let out a soft snort and pulled on his leash.

"What is it?" Jillian asked.

"I think they want to go. All righty then, let's head back to the stairs. Should we head up or ...? Wow, look at them go! Jillian? Are you coming?"

"I'm right behind you."

We emerged onto the main floor and were immediately pulled back to the control room. Dr. Rozhkov was still there, talking with Chris and several of the animal keepers. Katia and Penny were back, having finished their searches of whatever they were assigned to investigate. Siggie, we were told, was stuck at home, caring for a sick family member. We weren't told who.

"Where'd Shannon go?" Jillian asked.

Surprised, Marianne scanned the room. Sure enough, her assistant was nowhere to be found.

"She was just here, like two minutes ago. Shannon? Are you here?" There was no answer. "Shannon? Where did that girl go? Let me give her a call. She always … hmm. It went straight to voice mail. Something is going on. Chris, can you review the video footage and tell me when and where Shannon disappeared to?"

The computer tech nodded and started typing so fast that his fingers became a blur. I had to take my hat off to the guy. I was a writer by trade, but there was no way I could come anywhere close to matching that guy's speed on a computer.

"Found her," he reported, several minutes later. "You'd better get over here. You're gonna want to see this."

We all crowded around the large display.

"What did you find?" Dr. Rozhkov asked. "Where is she?"

"She's no longer on site," Chris reported. "She left the moment Zack and Jillian headed downstairs. Coincidence?"

"I feel obligated to say no," Marianne decided. "Why did she leave? What did you two do down there?"

"We just sat and talked," Jillian said. "That's all, I

swear."

"What does she know that we don't?" I asked, growing interested. "She clearly thinks we were up to something, and whatever it was, she didn't want to stick around to find out." I looked at my dogs and shook my head. Had they heard me complain that we didn't have a prime suspect yet? Is this their way of giving me a hint? "Doc? How well do you know your assistant?"

"I thought I knew her better than most," Marianne replied. After a few moments, she sighed. "But, I'm guessing I really didn't know her at all. Do you think Shannon had something to do with the theft of our chick?"

Jillian pointed straight down.

"She thought we were doing something. It frightened her so badly she felt she had to flee. So, does anyone else wonder what might be found down there?"

I squatted next to the dogs.

"Let's find out, shall we? Guys, it's time to impress me. I know you can do it, but it's time to show everyone here how good you guys really are. You need to earn that stellar reputation of yours. There's something downstairs that Shannon believes we found. We need you guys to find it for us."

Sherlock rose to his feet, stretched his back, and then wiggled his rear in a very encouraging manner, as if to say he was up for the challenge. Watson also stretched, but the only other thing we got out of her was a token of her appreciation: a reminder she suffers from flatulence. In layman's terms, she farted.

I heard Chris chuckle.

"Wow, she's worse than my father, and that's saying something."

"Damn, Watson," I laughed, waving a hand through the air in an attempt to fan it away from me, "that's a ripe one. Holy cow. You'd think she ate nothing but junk food."

"She doesn't, does she?" Chris asked, in a soft voice.

"Of course not," I said. "She just, well, eats too fast. Guys? Lead the way."

Sherlock hurried out of the room, making a beeline straight for the stairs leading down. Whatever had attracted his attention was lost on Watson. My little girl made it to the top of the steps and looked down at the imposing flight of stairs leading down. If I didn't know any better, I'd swear I heard her groan.

Smiling to myself, I scooped my red and white girl up in my arms and headed downstairs. I also noticed that I had an audience tagging along. Marianne, Chris, Katia, and Penny were following from a distance. Once we were back in the small sitting area, I noticed Sherlock was waiting at the locked door leading into CCCP's infirmary.

"Do you have a key?" I asked Dr. Rozhkov, as she stepped up to the door.

Marianne fished out her key chain and held up a

single, golden key.

"Please. I have the God key. This unlocks every single lock in this place. Sherlock. Watson. After you."

The corgis strutted their way through the door, but as soon as they were inside, both came to an immediate halt. Sherlock's nose dropped to the floor and he sniffed a few times. Watson looked back at me, as if to verify I was still there.

"Find whatever Shannon was nervous about," I ordered.

"You're assuming there was," Chris said.

I felt the leashes go taut. Sherlock had decided to head left, toward a large walk-in freezer. I remember seeing that behemoth the day we had our tour, and I don't remember anything standing out about it. Then again, we were never shown what was inside, either.

"What's in there?" I asked. "Come to think of it, why do you guys need such a large freezer in here?"

"The equipment was purchased by recommendation of an outside agency," Marianne answered. "For the record, I didn't think we needed something that large in here, either. Right now, we use it to store extra cases of fish. Zack, would you do the honors?"

"As long as a Yeti isn't going to jump out at me, sure."

"Use those gloves," Jillian urged, as she pointed at a pair of thick, fur-lined gloves hanging from a magnetic hook near a clipboard, hanging from a similar hook. A heavy, winter coat was also nearby. "We don't know how cold it gets in there."

I nodded. "Got it. For that matter, I think I'll borrow that coat. If I'm going to be poking around, I'd rather not come out as a popsicle."

Properly attired, I took several steps into the freezer when I came to an abrupt stop. Holy freakin' moley, it was cold in here. My breath looked like a thick jet of smoke, which briefly reminded me of the dragon link to this case. Looking around, I saw stacks and stacks of flat cardboard boxes, which I recognized as boxes of smelt and krill from the kitchen freezers. Marianne was right. Metal shelves were installed on two of the walls, and they were mostly empty. Aside from the four pallets of fish, there really wasn't anything in here. Turning, I made for the door. I don't know what the dogs thought was in here, but there really wasn't any … wait. What was that?

Wedged between two stacks of frozen slabs of krill was something brown. Was it paper? Some leftover trash?

I managed to pry the object loose and, without waiting to see what it was, made for the door. Once outside, Chris helped me push the heavy metal door closed. Jillian made it to my side first.

"Zachary? Are you okay?"

"Y-yeah." When did my teeth start rattling? "I th-think I f-found s-something."

I held up the wadded something-or-other and

gave it to Marianne, who took the item and, taking my gloves from me, gently smoothed out the crumpled item.

It was a small brown duffel bag.

"It is bag, *da*?" I heard Katia ask.

"*Da*," I returned, which earned me a smile from the Russian keeper.

"What's in it?" Jillian asked.

It took a few minutes for Dr. Rozhkov to work the zipper open, but when she was finally able to see inside, she gasped with shock. She gingerly reached inside and fumbled around a bit before pulling her gloved hand out. The rest of us crowded around as she opened her hand. On her palm were several shards of a greenish-white substance.

"Egg shells," Jillian whispered, shocked. "What are the remnants of egg shells doing in the freezer?"

Marianne looked up, at the two animal keepers.

"Didn't you two say that the egg shells were missing from our one hatched egg?"

"*Da*," Katia said. "Never found shell."

"I just assumed someone threw them away," Penny added.

"Which is strictly against protocol," Marianne said, growing angry.

"Shannon is the one who stole the chick!" Chris said, amazed. "I never would have believed it."

"So, the theft of the chick was an inside job after all," I said. "And, I'm sorry to say, Shannon was the inside man. Er, woman."

"I'm calling the police," Marianne said, as she reached for her phone. "If she's the one caring for the chick, then it must be at her place. I want them over there, now, before it's too late."

While Dr. Rozhkov placed the call, and explained the urgency of the situation, the rest of us huddled together.

"Who among us believes Shannon could be responsible for the theft?" I asked. Much to my surprise, every hand was raised. Well, I didn't see that coming. "How long has she worked here, does anyone know?"

Jillian closed her eyes and tried to think.

"I know she mentioned it earlier. Whether it was right or not remains to be seen."

"A month?" I guessed.

"Months," Jillian corrected. "She said she's been here for two months."

"She did?" I asked. "When did she say that?"

"When we were checking out the IP addresses. Remember Virginia? She said she didn't recognize any of us, and that included Shannon."

"I know who you're talking about," Chris said. The young tech was frowning as he wandered off. "She couldn't identify an IP address from a router if it had labels on it."

I detected movement in my peripheral vision. Sherlock, who had been reclining at my feet, had spotted Chris heading toward the main computer and was watching him intently.

"Shannon is the least of our worries right now," Chris added, his face grim. "Dr. Rozhkov, you're going to want to see this. Something tells me I need to bring up the CBS newsfeed."

CCCP's computer tech expertly tapped in a flurry of commands on the keyboard. The large video screen went black, and then a normal computer desktop appeared, albeit on a much larger scale. A browser window opened, and a website was entered.

The webpage for Sitka's one and only affiliated television network appeared. Local headlines were splayed across the front, with a healthy amount of animated ads interspersed here and there, displaying topics ranging from the impending arrival of winter to a special happening at the town's grocery store advertising locally grown meat. Important side note: it didn't identify the *source* of the meat. However, front and center on the page, in a font large enough to warrant a double-line display, was *PENGUIN PROBLEMS?* in upper-case letters.

"Oh, that's just great," Marianne groaned. "What's it say?"

Chris skimmed the article.

"Let's see. A report has surfaced that some type of crime has happened onsite at CCCP. Specialists were brought in to investigate, and since nothing has been confirmed, a news crew has been dispatched. It promises a live feed just as soon as the crew is on scene."

"A news crew?" Marianne repeated, appalled. "Here? Oh, this can't be happening!"

Chris pushed away from the keyboard and hurried off, without a word. We eyed each other, uncertain what he was doing. A few moments later, the facility's tech guru was back, this time holding a hand-held police scanner. He set it on the counter, made a few adjustments to the controls, and leaned back in his chair with a look of alarm on his face.

"You just so happened to have a police scanner with you?" Dr. Rozhkov asked.

"I like listening to their calls," Chris admitted.

"What calls?" I asked. "I don't hear anything."

Right on cue, a voice appeared, asking for the status of a records check from a few minutes ago. The next several minutes passed in silence before the display switched to the numerous video feeds. Chris selected one, and the feed rapidly expanded to fit the display. We were now looking at a live shot of the circular driveway out front. There, parked near CCCP's front door, was the news van, complete with the extendible antenna on its top. A pile of gear was rapidly growing as the aforementioned news crew unloaded the van. Dr. Rozhkov sighed and sank down into the closest chair.

"I have no idea what to tell them. None. If word of this leaks out, then we can kiss that accreditation goodbye. This is the end of CCCP, I'm afraid. I'm sorry, everyone. I'm so very sorry. I thought we could keep this under wraps."

Jillian raised a hand. "Marianne, perhaps we could help?"

I turned to my wife with a look of skepticism on my face.

"And what are we going to be able to do?"

Jillian ignored my question.

"Would you like us to handle this? After all, Zachary is an expert in dealing with news crews."

Had I been drinking *anything*, I would have snotted it across the room, I'm sure.

"Excuse me? I am?"

"Who among us has told a group of news reporters to vacate the premises on more than one occasion?" Jillian countered.

"I had Vance backing me up," I reminded her.

My wife stared at me for a few moments, and then batted her eyes.

"Fine," I groaned. "I'll see what I can do."

I handed her the leashes to the dogs as I passed by.

"Good afternoon," a smartly dressed guy in his late twenties told me, as I exited CCCP's front door. "For the record, please, will you state your name?"

"You're polite," I decided. "I'll try to reciprocate. You're trespassing. I need you and your team to pack up and clear out. There's nothing to report here."

"I'm sorry, fella," the young guy smirked, "but this is public land. I have every right to be here. Now, will you please identify yourself, or should I just call you Mr. John Doe?"

"Mr. John Doe is fine," I said, keeping a smile on my face. "And you are …?"

"Chadwick Festerworth, Channel Seven news. Now, will …"

I pulled out my phone. "Chadwick Festerworth, from the local news channel. Got it. Just a moment, while I call the police."

"This is public land," the reporter insisted.

I pointed at the mailbox at the street, nearly several hundred feet away.

"See the mailbox? That's where the mail is delivered. Now, would you care to ask why it's all the way over there?"

The smugness vanished.

"Oh, uh …"

"That's where you'll find the road. The *public* road. You and your crew are trespassing on private property. You've got thirty seconds to load your gear and get your tails past that mailbox. Otherwise, I've got you on video, and you guys will probably be featured as the top news story on your own broadcast. It's up to you."

"Fine," the reporter grumped, as he stomped back to his van. "You have to give us longer than thirty seconds."

"You're down to twenty," I advised, looking at my watch. I held up my phone and showed them the emergency number already entered into my phone. All I had to do was hit the *Dial* button.

The speed with which the team of three

dismantled their setup surprised me. Wow, those suckers could move if properly motivated. They had everything stowed and the van moved *past* the mailbox with five seconds to spare. Nodding, I was about to head back inside when a sound stopped me in my tracks.

It was a very recognizable hum from an engine, and it was coming from above. Was that a plane? Wasn't there supposed to be a temporary ban on flying in or out of town at the moment?

Something was wrong. There shouldn't be anything in the air. This had to mean something. Hurrying back inside, I sought out Dr. Rozhkov and pulled her aside.

"Did you get them to leave?" Marianne asked, amazed. "You're going to have to teach me how to handle those …"

"I'm sorry to interrupt," I began, "but didn't you say that your contact at the police department confirmed all planes had been grounded?"

"Yes, why?"

"Either you were lied to, or else I just saw someone who blatantly disregarded the rules. One of those pontoon planes just flew over us."

Dr. Rozhkov frowned. "Directly over us? You're sure?"

"Yes, why?" I asked.

"It's an agreement we have with the tourism board, and the local airport. Excessive noise and frequent crossings by planes have been known to upset animals in zoos, so most cities declare the space over their zoos as no-fly zones. To see a plane fly over us, it has to be related to what's been happening here. I don't suppose it was low enough to make out the plane's tail number, was it?'

"I'm sorry," I said, shaking my head. "The only thing I could make out was the color. Bright yellow." Sherlock's head lifted. He looked right at me and snorted with exasperation. "Like … like …"

"… a banana?" Marianne finished for me. Her eyes narrowed, and her brow creased. "Is the rear of the plane black? Just the tip, mind you."

I brought up an image of the plane in my head. Yes, there it was. The plane's tail fins were black, and the main body of the plane was yellow, just like a flippin' banana.

"I'll be a monkey's uncle," I breathed.

"It's a very well-known plane in town," Chris explained. "It gets the most tourists, 'cause it's always flying someone somewhere. With that color, you can't miss it."

"I just figured it was part of a fleet of planes," I said. "I mean, I've seen it around town, too. Sherlock even had me take a picture of it."

We all stared at the corgis.

"I think we need to look into whoever owns that plane," Jillian said.

Marianne was already holding her cell to her ear.

"I'm way ahead of you. Marianne Rozhkov for Detective Kevin Taneidí, please."

While Marianne relayed our newest discovery to the police, Jillian and I, and the dogs, headed for the closest set of chairs. I pulled my phone out to peruse all the corgi clues pictures one more time.

"Bananas," I was saying. "Could it be the reason the dogs have been fixating on everyone's favorite yellow fruit? Because of that plane?"

"That's hard to say," Jillian admitted. "After all, what dog doesn't love a chunk of banana? No, before you remind me, I'm well aware of Sherlock and Watson's refusal to eat their piece until you snapped a picture. Very well, let's assume we're correct. Bananas are a reference to that plane. Well, what do we do about it?"

"What *can* we do about it?" I countered. "It's not like we have friends in the police department here."

Marianne appeared. "Bruce Smith."

"Who's Bruce Smith?" I wanted to know.

"The owner and operator of the Banana Boat float plane. We need to tread carefully. Detective Taneidí said that Mr. Smith's history with the town runs long and deep. He's been a respected businessman for over twenty years, and has lived here in town for nearly double that."

"Does he have any motivation to pull something like this off?" I asked. I detected movement and glanced down. Sherlock and Watson had sunk into *down* positions and were watching us closely.

"There aren't any priors," Marianne reported. "Not so much as a speeding ticket. I'm thinking we shouldn't accuse Mr. Smith unless we have irrefutable proof of his guilt."

"What, two corgis insisting he's connected to a crime isn't good enough for the local police department?" I chuckled. "Besides, the name Bruce Smith? It sounds fairly generic, like someone made it up."

"It's not," Marianne said, shaking her head. "I haven't even been in town that long and I've heard of him. Chris, you said you've lived here for several years. What do you think? Have you heard of him? Chris?"

I automatically looked back at the desk with the master computer. The chair was empty and still spinning, as if the occupant had beat a hasty retreat. Sherlock and Watson instantly looked left, toward the main entrance. A feeling of urgency washed through me. Without announcing what I was doing, I hurried for the foyer. Chris was there, hastily donning his winter coat. But, as he was hurrying, his sleeve must have caught on something inside the coat, resulting in a section of his left arm becoming exposed. I sucked in a breath as I realized what I was looking at.

"Oh, Zack. You startled me. I didn't see you there."

"Going somewhere?" I inquired, fighting hard to keep my tone upbeat. "You seem to be in a hurry."

"Nah, I just realized I left something in my car. I think Dr. Rozhkov needs to see it."

"Is that so? What is it?"

"I'll show you. Give me a moment, would you?"

"Nice tattoo," I said, and pointed at the exposed

patch of skin on his left arm. "What is that coiled around your arm?"

"Oh, this? It's nothing."

"Kinda looks like a dragon," I said, giving him a knowing smirk.

"It's actually something called a wyverian."

"Which is just another way of saying it's a two-legged dragon," I replied. "Hey, I enjoy reading fantasy books, too, and know all about those overgrown reptiles. You know what? You're right. I think Dr. Rozhkov definitely needs to see that."

Chris stifled a curse and hurried out the door, not bothering to close it behind him.

"What was that all about?" Jillian asked, appearing next to me.

I closed the door and hooked a thumb at it.

"Chris just split. Guess what? He had a tattoo on his arm. A dragon. Come on, we need to tell Dr. Rozhkov."

"What? Chris is our culprit? But ... what about Shannon? And this Bruce Smith character?"

I sighed and looked at my corgis.

"From no suspects to three in less than two hours. That's gotta be a record, even for them."

TEN

D o you really think this is going to work?" Jillian asked, nearly an hour later. "Granted, Sitka isn't that big, but this is a stretch, even for them."

"Now who's the skeptic?" I asked my wife, as we slowly made the turn onto Lincoln Street. We were now passing through the downtown district. "They've done stuff like this before. I trust the dogs. If anyone can find these guys, it's them."

"Your faith has been restored," Jillian said, smiling. "I'm so glad, Zachary."

"I never should have doubted them. Everything always ties together. Always! Although, I will admit that I'm still not sure how Shannon, Chris, and this Bruce fellow are connected. I can only assume we'll find that out later."

"Do you really think we'll find something on that street with the fallen tree?" my wife asked.

"Someone wanted to make sure we weren't able to pursue the Mustang, so I figure it's the best place to start. If they're still in town, then that'd be where I would look."

"You're assuming they haven't found a way out of town," Jillian said.

"True. I can only go off of what we were told. We saw the yellow plane, so we know he isn't driving. If both methods have been locked down, then that has to mean they're still here. You're right. Sitka is small. It wouldn't take that long to cruise through every street there is, but I'm thinking we won't have to. I think if we can get close enough, then our two wonder dogs will take care of the rest."

"How are the roads?"

"I won't lie, they're a little slick," I reported. "Then again, what do you expect? It snowed a few more inches today."

"At least the roads are plowed," Jillian added.

"But not before the locals drove over it first and compacted it," I said, through gritted teeth. "There are patches of ice and packed snow everywhere. It's a good thing we're not in a high-speed pursuit. It'd be the world's slowest, and that's saying something after we had the infamous Scooter Chase last year."

We were in the same white van that had picked us up from the airport several days ago. This time, however, I was behind the wheel, since Shannon had vanished yesterday. For that matter, so had Chris. I was beginning to think they were, er, cahooting? Er, cahooters? In cahoots? Oh, I know. Colluding. The two of them were colluding together. I just wished I knew why. It might help us figure out what those two were planning. Before I forget, I should mention we have a third no-show: one Mr. Bruce Smith. A detective went out to his house to get a statement, but he and his plane had vanished. In addition, the pier where he tied up his plane was currently empty, and we were told it had been that way for the past day or two. What was his role in the theft of the penguin? And most importantly, was he working with both Shannon and Chris?

"It's amazing to see how many people are on the road," my wife commented, drawing me out of my reverie. "If I personally see snow on the ground, then I can guarantee you I'm not driving anywhere."

"This is probably nothing to them," I said, as I turned right, to continue driving along the waterfront. "A few inches is child's play compared to the estimated five feet of snow that's clearly on the way. Which way now?"

Jillian consulted the map.

"Left. Turn left here, which will lead us to Sawmill Creek Road. Then, we turn right. That'll take us east, to the edge of town. We want Shotgun, which will be on the right."

We drove in silence for another five minutes before I got the first sign from the corgis. Sherlock, who had been snoozing on a pile of blankets in the cargo section of the van, suddenly awoke and was trying to wiggle his way onto Jillian's lap. My wife flipped the arm rest up and picked Sherlock up.

She was rewarded with a friendly lick to her chin before he turned to watch the passing scenery.

As we approached the turnoff for Shotgun Street, Sherlock looked right.

"Right it is. Glad you agree, pal. Hang on, it's a little steep here. I'm going to go as slow as I can. Are there any outlets or does this street dead-end?"

"There are a couple of smaller streets," Jillian reported. "One, two, three … looks like three."

We passed the first, and I nodded. The name started with a K, but there was no way I'd be able to pronounce it. True to Jillian's word, the small street looked like a dirt path compared to Sawmill Creek. Shotgun was only wide enough to allow a single car to pass. Just ahead, visible now as a series of cut chunks of tree trunks, laid the pieces of the fallen tree from yesterday. Or was it the day before? The days were beginning to blur together. Anyway, someone had cleared the road, but only by slicing up the wood and pushing it off, to the side. I was honestly surprised someone hadn't claimed the wood, seeing how everyone in town had wood burning fireplaces.

"Is he still with us?" Jillian suddenly asked.

I checked my rearview mirror and nodded. "Officer Sanderson is still there."

Three car-lengths behind us was a four-wheel-drive SUV, with the word POLICE emblazoned on all sides. The local police, at Marianne's request, dispatched a unit to keep an eye on us, in case someone was waiting to ambush us. The last thing either of us wanted was trouble, and let's face it, there was a better-than-average chance we were about to stick our noses where they didn't belong. After all, we already had a tree dropped in front of us. How do we know our adversary wouldn't resort to something similar, should the situation arise?

Right on cue, my phone rang. Placing the call on speaker, I took the call.

"Officer Sanderson. Glad to see you still back there."

"Call me Ron. Where are we headed, Mr. Anderson?"

"If I call you Ron, you have to call me Zack."

We both heard some laughter.

"Fair enough. Where are we going?"

"This is the road we were on before, when we lost the Mustang," I reported, driving slowly. The police SUV was less than twenty feet behind me. "See those logs over there? That's what's left of the tree that was blocking the road."

"You think the perp is somewhere around here?" Ron asked.

"I do. If not this street, then somewhere nearby. I'm hoping the dogs will tell me where."

"And they've done this before?" Ron skeptically asked.

"On quite a few occasions," I confirmed. "And before you ask, yes, it's worked every time, and no, I don't have a clue how they do it."

"Roger that."

"Been living in town long?" I asked, several

minutes later.

"Five years," Ron told me. "My girlfriend and I took an Alaskan cruise, and we both fell in love with the town the moment we stepped off the ship."

"That's sweet," Jillian added, raising her voice.

"Mrs. Anderson," Ron acknowledged.

"Please. It's Jillian."

"Yes, ma'am."

"Yikes. Don't call me ma'am."

"Yes, ma'am. Oh, er, sorry."

Our vehicles approached the second side street. A tiny road branched southwest, and disappeared into the trees. A quick glance at the dogs confirmed we wouldn't be turning on that road any time soon.

"What's your girlfriend do for a living, Ron?" Jillian asked.

"She's a teacher at the middle school. Math. She loves working with numbers."

"Any kids?" Jillian wanted to know.

"No. Not planning on any, to tell the truth. There is no better contraceptive than having to take care of a roomful of kids day in and day out."

We rounded a corner and I saw another intersection approaching. This time, the road branched to the right, and looked as though it might run along the water.

"Does either of you have any family in town?" I asked, as I automatically slowed, while keeping an eye on Sherlock and Watson. So far, neither had perked up.

"My girlfriend's family is from Juneau," Ron reported. "Mine are in Arizona."

I perked up. "Oh, yeah? I used to live in Phoenix. Whereabouts?"

"Cave Creek. Know where it is?"

"I do," I confirmed. "Cave Creek is a really cool town north of Phoenix. It has some great restaurants, and a fantastic section of gift shops running along an old-fashioned boardwalk."

"That's it, exactly. My parents are retired, and keep trying to get us to move there."

"You'd have to really love the heat," I said. "It gets brutal there during the summer. Honestly? I don't miss it."

As we neared the intersection, I saw that the sign read Islander. I was about to announce our arrival when both dogs perked up. The corgis, being unable to see out a window, huffed irritably. Then, and this really shouldn't surprise me, Sherlock looked left, which happened to be the direction to go in order to turn onto this newest street.

"And we're turning. Ron, keep your eyes open. The dogs are now awake and are paying attention."

"Copy that, Zack. Perhaps I should take the lead?"

"Does Islander have any side streets?"

"No. It runs through Harris Island. People have their own private launches there, so you'll find tons of boats."

"Private launches," I repeated. "What about planes? Could someone park a plane there?"

"They're not supposed to," Ron informed us. "There are regulations which prevent a floater from taking off near residential properties."

There were a few houses on either side of the street, with the south side being closest to the water. We slowed to a crawl and kept a close eye on the corgis. Sherlock and Watson were both on their feet, staring up at us. What did it mean? We had to go straight ahead?

"Keep an eye on them," I said, as I continued to allow the van to roll forward. "We've got a few houses coming up on the right. Maybe one of those?"

"Anything?" I heard Ron ask. Apparently, I'd left the call connected.

"Not yet. I will mention that we could be stopping at a moment's notice. Since you're here, and if we just so happen to find something, be prepared to act. The last thing our suspect is going to want to see is a cop car pull up to their house."

"I read you," Ron said. "I'll be ready."

We followed the street for another couple of minutes when we finally encountered some signs of life. A person was walking on the right-hand sidewalk, headed in the same direction as we were. Since it was below freezing outside, the individual was wearing a thick gray coat, with the hood pulled up, and a black set of earmuffs.

"*Woof.*"

Jillian immediately turned to look at the dogs. Sherlock and Watson only had eyes for the walker on the side of the street.

"I heard that," Ron reported. "What are they looking at? The woman?"

To best describe what happened next, we'd have to slow time to a crawl.

I answered, stating I didn't see anyone else, so it had to be the same person. The dogs lost their freaking minds, which made Ron ask me to repeat what I said, and the dude walking in front of us finally turned around. Ron's guess to the gender was right.

"There's only one person out here," I said.

Both corgis began barking, which naturally drowned me out.

"I didn't copy," Ron said.

The person with the gray coat turned. We all caught sight of the blonde hair. She locked eyes on me and froze, like a deer in a set of headlights. Then, she saw the police car directly behind me. She let out a blood-curdling shriek of dismay and immediately sprinted down someone's side yard and disappeared.

"That was Shannon!" Jillian exclaimed. "Ron, do you copy? That was Shannon Silverman. She was the first person to vanish from CCCP!"

"I just radioed it in," Ron said, growing excited. "Those dogs are amazing. Can you tell where she went?"

"Through the side yard between the white

Victorian and the light blue ranch home," I reported. "Looks like she's headed for the water. Unless she has a boat, I have no idea where she's going."

"Wait here," Ron ordered. "Islander is only a few hundred feet long. There's no outlet. We're to wait for backup."

"Got it. We're pulling off to the side."

Sitka's finest were there in less than two minutes. It didn't take long to track down the unfortunate Ms. Silverman. When she appeared, handcuffed, with a cop on either arm, her face was the complete opposite of the last time I saw her. Her eyes were wild and defiant, and her face was a mask of pure anger and hate. She looked my way, shot daggers from her eyes, and lifted her chin, as though I was no longer worthy to breathe the same air.

A uniformed policeman approached our van and knocked on the window. I bumped the heater up to full and rolled the window down.

"Detective Kevin Taneidí, Sitka Police. You must be Mr. Zachary Anderson. And Mrs. Anderson, I presume?"

I shook the proffered hand. "We are. It's good to meet you, Detective. Has Shannon said anything to you?"

"Nothing I'm willing to repeat in the presence of a lady," the detective returned. We all heard Sherlock snort with irritation. The corgis hadn't been included with the introductions, and

Sherlock was moments away from voicing his displeasure. Thankfully, Detective Taneidí leaned forward just a bit and saw Sherlock and Watson returning his frank stare. "And these must be the famous corgis I've heard so much about. Well, you pups found one of the three we're searching for. Care to find the other two?"

"*WOOF!*" Sherlock was bouncing up and down on his two front paws.

I had only seen him do that when I was playing with a toy he really wanted.

"You have got his attention," I chuckled.

"We're going to pull back," Taneidí explained. "In case they find something else, we don't want to alert them to our presence, not that they probably haven't already figured something is up."

I pointed at the two houses I could see. Both were on a small ridge, which then sloped down to the water. Those two houses must be worth a fortune to have such spectacular views.

"Do we know who lives there?"

Ron shrugged. "I don't, no. Should I find out?"

"It couldn't hurt," I said. "Shannon was fleeing somewhere. It'd make sense she'd choose a familiar house. It'd be nice to know if one of those houses belonged to a Silverman."

"Gotcha. Let me call it in."

We had our answer in less than thirty seconds. For the second time, we were asked to fall back. Why? The large ranch-style house we could see in the distance belonged to a familiar name, and that was only because he happened to own a bright yellow airplane. It belonged to none other than Bruce Smith. What, then, was Shannon doing running to that house? Did they know each other?

We didn't get a chance to discuss the ramifications. The garage door exploded outward and we all heard the roar of a super-charged engine, screaming in rage. The dark green Mustang raced down the driveway, almost striking two police officers, who were slowly approaching the house. The sports car turned left onto Islander Street, and from the sounds of the engine, whoever was driving must've stomped on the accelerator. The only problem was, it was headed straight for us, and I had yet to clear out of its way.

"It's coming for us!" Jillian shrieked, throwing up her hands, as if to find some way to brace herself for the impending collision.

Thankfully, the car rocketed by us and disappeared up the road. It might have been traveling close to a hundred miles an hour, but it was still enough time for me to identify the driver: Chris. CCCP's former computer tech had a look of sheer terror on his face as he went by. From the direction the car was headed, he appeared to be heading back to town, which was probably the stupidest thing he could have done. He wasn't going to make it far. In less time than it takes to come up with a few choice swear words, four Sitka police cars were on his tail. And, let's face it, there was nowhere for him to go.

Before we knew it, we were alone on Islander Court, with Bruce Smith's house visible before us. Everything happened so fast that I didn't even have time to put the van in park. Once it was, Jillian and I shared a look before we burst out laughing.

"First Shannon, and now Chris," I said, shaking my head.

"And they were found at Bruce Smith's house," Jillian added. "They *must* know each other. I just wish we knew how. What now? Should we follow?"

I shrugged, put the van into gear, and was in the process of looking for a safe place to turn around when I noticed the dogs. Sherlock and Watson were staring, transfixed, at Bruce Smith's house. If Chris was gone, and Shannon had been arrested, did that mean Bruce was somewhere inside?

"Is Ron still out there?" I quietly asked.

Jillian turned in her seat to check the area.

"I think so. I see an SUV off to the side of the road. He called you, so his number should be in your cell. Can you call him?"

"I suppose."

"Zachary, why aren't you calling?"

I unhooked my seat belt.

"It couldn't hurt to look, could it?"

In a move so smooth, so fluid, that it made my mind spin, my darling wife caught the seat belt's fastener as it was released and quickly snapped it back into place.

"Oh, no you don't. You're staying put. He could be armed. He could've laid a trap. You're not going to risk yourself."

"Fine. And holy cow, by the way. Nice catch! When did you become a ninja?" Ron's number was located, and then dialed. "Ron, is that your car, still on Islander?"

"Yeah, it is. By the way, I just received word: the driver of the Mustang was apprehended. Our two suspects will now be sharing a cell. I'd love to be a fly on that wall. What's up?"

"Sherlock and Watson are staring at that house and haven't blinked once. I think there still might be someone in there."

"Your dogs have earned their reputations," Ron said, his voice becoming firm. "If they want a second look at that house, then what could it hurt?"

The SUV's door opened and Ron emerged, holding the phone to his ear.

"But, don't we need a warrant to be able to see inside the house?" I protested.

"A suspect fled from that residence," Officer Sanderson explained, "and one was apprehended nearby. It's now a crime scene. That's why I'm still here. I get to make sure no one messes with the house until the C.S.I. techs arrive. What's the matter? Do you guys want to check it out? If so, you can, only this is the part where I say not to touch anything, but something tells me you already knew that."

"Yeppers. All right, we're headed your way."

Once the dogs and I were standing outside the van, and Jillian was now seated behind the wheel—just in case—we followed Officer Ronald Sanderson to the front door. He was about to reach for the door knob when I saw him lean forward and listen intently for a few moments. He tried the handle, only it was locked.

I pointed at the garage. "We've got a pretty big hole over there to walk through. Chris left it nice and open for us."

Ron nodded and together we walked through the shattered remains of the house's double-wide garage. There was a third garage, on the right. There weren't any vehicles parked there, but it was full. Of junk. Two engines, swinging on hoists, racks and racks of tools, and various parts were everywhere. I recognized an impressive collection of distributor caps, three or four car batteries, a stack of snow tires, and a half-built carburetor.

The first thing we saw that indicated we were in the right place was a set of airplane propellers hanging from the wall on a set of hooks, just like you would with a set of screwdrivers. A yellow pontoon was standing on end in the corner, and a small, padded seat—with the upholstery peeling off in stages—was propped up next to it.

Ron turned to me, forked a couple of fingers at his eyes, and then pointed at a small set of stairs, leading up to a solid brown door. His palm opened and he patted the air, indicating I should wait.

The officer reached for the door knob when we all heard a distinctive crash come from somewhere within the house. Then, a loud curse and running footsteps.

Ron grunted irritably, drew his weapon, and yanked the door open. The dogs and I shared a look and waited for permission to enter. I may be a paid police consultant back home, but here in Alaska we were still tourists. Plus, the last thing I wanted to do was put myself, or the dogs, in any type of danger. I'd never do that to Jillian.

Ron called out twice, identifying himself. Naturally, there was no answer. Then, I heard several shouts, and then Ron's rang out loud and clear.

"Halt! You're under arrest! Get on the ground, now! There's no point running, Smith! We've got ... dammit!"

That prompted me to duck inside. Wow. It looked as though a cyclone had touched down. Furniture was upended. Pictures lay inside their broken frames on the floor. Cabinets had been yanked open, and the fridge door was still ajar.

I noticed bits of broken glass on the floor and gently steered the dogs around the mess. A glass sliding door was open, and through it I could see a clear path all the way down to a private pier. Unfortunately, I could also see a very distinctive yellow pontoon plane pulling away from the shore. The single-prop floater revved its engine and, moments later, lifted off the water, only to disappear into the cloudy sky.

"Damn," Ron swore. "I had him. I didn't think he'd abandon his house. He seemed reluctant to leave, but only did so once he saw me."

Together, we looked back at the house. Sherlock and Watson pulled on their leashes, eager to head inside. Because it was cold or was it because they picked up on something they wanted us to find?

"Go ahead, guys. You've earned it. What do you want to look at?"

While Ron radioed in the events that had happened, I gave the corgis some extra slack in their leashes and let them lead. We returned to the living room and while I was contemplating what to do, heard Sherlock whine.

"I'm surprised, boy. You typically howl at me when you want me to do something. What is it? What do you want me to see?"

The dogs guided me to a hallway on the left. Glancing inside each open doorway as we passed, verifying nothing was going to jump out at us, we saw several bedrooms, a study, and the master suite. All of which, I might add, had been tossed. If I didn't know any better, I'd say ol' Bruce had misplaced something, and he was hoping he could find it before he was forced to leave town.

"Do you smell that?" Ron asked, alarmed.

I sniffed the air. Uh, oh. Rotten eggs assailed my nostrils. Gas! Natural gas, to be precise. Had he left a burner on?

"We need to clear out of here," Ron snapped. "If

there's the slightest spark, then this whole place will be turned into a raging inferno. For all we know, that could be Smith's plan. Get your dogs and make for the door. Hurry!"

I wasn't going to wait for a second opinion. I wrapped Sherlock and Watson's leashes tightly around my hand and hurriedly retraced our steps, back to the garage, when my arm was violently yanked backwards. It felt as though I had just tied my arm to a telephone pole and tried to yank it out with brute force.

"Ow! Come on, guys! This isn't the time to do this. We need to clear out before ..."

"Awwwoooowoooowoooo!" Sherlock howled.

Both dogs turned completely around and headed the opposite direction, namely inside the house. Once they made it to the end of their leash, since I hadn't budged, they both looked at me and whined piteously.

"Guys? We don't have time for this! We've got to go!"

Sherlock and Watson refused. Ron gave me an exasperated look but finally nodded.

"Make it quick, Zack. Hurry! What do we need to see?"

We were taken past the kitchen and toward the hallway with doors on either side. Two were open, revealing the bedrooms I had noticed before. That left two doors, both of which turned out to be closets. I was closing the second when Sherlock leapt forward, wedging his body in the doorway.

"What are you doing? Come on, pal. We've got to clear out!"

"Awwoooo!" Sherlock argued.

"Ooooo!" Watson added, in her own version of a howl.

Sighing loudly, I pulled Sherlock out of the closet and took stock of what was in there. For the record, not much. There were a couple of old green coats, the kind that look like they could've been purchased at a military supply store. A dilapidated vacuum cleaner was leaning against the closet wall. However, what got my attention were the footprints. Muddy prints on the floor, to be precise. The closet was small, and ordinarily wouldn't have bothered me, but what jumped out were the footprints. They extended to the back wall of the closet, and damned if it didn't look like one of the footprints was cut off in mid-step!

"Check it out," I said, nudging Ron. "Look at the prints. They go right up to the wall, and then it looks like they keep going."

Officer Sanderson reached in and knocked on the wall a few times. A hollow thump sounded, telling us exactly what we wanted to hear. There was something behind it!

"What do we have here?" Ron asked. He then coughed. "The fumes are getting worse. We need to speed this up. How do we get in?"

I looked down at the corgis.

"Sherlock? Watson? What do we do? How do we get in?"

Both dogs craned their heads to look up at me, and then looked left. Left? I ran my hands along the wall. Nothing. I then slid my hands under the only shelf in the closet, situated above eye-level. Still nothing. I looked back at the corgis, but both were still staring at the shelf. Hmm. The shelf *was* higher than I could see. Could there be something on the top side?

I placed my fingers on the top of the shelf and then repeated the motions. Sure enough, I felt a small, plastic cube with a recessed button. Once pressed, we heard a latch unclick and the entire closet wall swung away from me. It was a door! There was a hidden room back there!

I noticed the smell right away. Poo. Something was living back here, and whatever it was, it had been making a mess. I told myself this is what a chicken coop must smell like. And then, we heard it. A soft, high-pitched peep. Then another. It didn't take a degree in nuclear physics to identify the source of the sound. Suddenly, the peeps were coming so fast that I just knew the baby penguin had heard us, and was calling for help.

"Zack, we've got to get outta here!" Ron yelled. "Get in there, grab that thing, and let's go!"

I tossed the leashes to the officer and ducked into the tiny room. A small table, a pint-sized fridge, and a three-foot by two-foot wire folding dog kennel were instantly recognizable. There, in the kennel, was probably the cutest thing on two feet that I had ever seen. A fuzzy gray and white chick was peeping like crazy and rushing at the kennel, hoping to get out. Unsure what the protocol was for handling the chick, I smelled the first waft of gas coming inside the hidden room and gasped as I realized what Bruce was planning on doing.

The presence of the gas meant the plan was now to cut losses and cover his tracks. What was the best way to do that? Blow up his house and start over, presumably somewhere *else.* Unfortunately, that meant Bruce had signed the poor chick's death warrant.

Without thinking, I opened the kennel's gate and prepared to snatch the chick, only the baby penguin was amazingly agile. It darted between my legs and headed for the open closet door.

"This isn't the time to be doing this!" I yelled, as I turned to follow. I didn't make it far. The chick, much to my surprise, had stopped in front of Ron and was currently nuzzling the corgis. Sherlock, even more surprisingly, was nosing the fuzzy baby bird. "Sherlock? We've got to go! Get him to move, would you?"

Instead of guiding the chick outside, which is what I expected my two herding dogs to do, Sherlock instead nudged the fuzzy gray chick toward me. Recognizing what he wanted me to do, I scooped up the chick and stuffed it inside my sweatshirt.

"We're outta here. Move! Watson, keep up!"

"Go, go, go!" Ron was urging me.

He didn't need to ask twice. I took Sherlock and Watson's leash and made for the door. We had cleared the house, and were well on our way back to the van—and Officer Sanderson's police vehicle —when I thought for certain I had misinterpreted the presence of the gas. Maybe this wasn't a deliberate attack, or an act of sabotage. What we had here was …

WHOOM!

The house went up in a huge ball of fire. Plumes of smoke and flames shot dozens of feet skyward as the house exploded. Shards of glass, slivers of wood, and pretty much everything you'd expect were flung in all directions.

Jillian was out of the van in a flash.

"Zachary! Omigod! Are you okay? Officer Sanderson? What about you?"

Ron nodded. "We're good. Talk about in the nick of time. Had your dogs stalled us any longer, then we'd probably be well done by now."

"He meant for it to go up," I said, growing angry.

"Who?" Jillian asked.

"Bruce Smith. He set that gas on purpose."

Ron sobered. "You're sure, Zack? That's not a charge to make lightly."

"Why else would he flee?" I demanded. "He knew we were on to him. He had to cover his tracks or become implicated in the theft of the chick."

"That poor little baby," Jillian moaned. "I feel so bad for it. It didn't deserve to die like that."

I unzipped my sweatshirt. The chick,

apparently, had found a comfortable place to settle, and that was against my chest. Then again, I can see why. After all, to it, I'm just a walking hot water bottle. Jillian saw the chick huddled inside my coat and her eyes shot open. The chick, which had been sleeping, raised its head, looked at Jillian, and peeped a few times. Then the eyes closed and it promptly went back to sleep.

"You saved it! Oh my goodness, it's so cute! Look how adorable it is! How could anyone want to harm such a beautiful creature?"

I felt a tap on my shoulder. Turning, I came face-to-face with Officer Sanderson.

"Zack, I thought you might like to take a look at this."

"What is it?"

"Oh, just something I spotted."

The officer handed me a picture frame, one he must've taken from Bruce's house. In it was a family photograph. It showed a smiling man with a handlebar mustache fishing on a boat. Next to him were two laughing children: a young boy, and an older girl. And she was blonde.

"The children!" Jillian exclaimed. "Look at the children! It's Shannon and Chris. I had no idea they were siblings! That means ..."

"They're one big happy family," I concluded. "It'll work out well for them. Maybe they can all serve time in the same cell."

Sherlock stretched his neck up. He wanted to see the picture. Holding the frame down low,

Sherlock's long snout nudged the photograph and then he brought his nose into contact with the glass.

"He touched the picture of Bruce," I said, shrugging. "Thanks, pal. We already know he's the one who … well, I'll be a monkey's uncle."

"What is it?" Jillian asked.

I flipped the frame around so that my two companions could see it.

"What is Bruce wearing?"

Jillian leaned forward.

"Looks like a flannel shirt, jeans, and boots. Why do you ask, Zachary?"

"Look at his head," I instructed. "What do you see?"

My wife's eyes widened.

"It's a baseball cap. What of it? Oh. Oh! Look! It has a moose on it!"

ELEVEN

T his can't be happening," we heard, as I used my access card to unlock CCCP's front door. Dr. Rozhkov was there, and she was pacing back and forth. "The inspector arrives tomorrow, we were sabotaged by our own computer tech, and my assistant is the one who walked our chick right through the front door. And what happens when we finally track down what happened to our chick? The house blows up, thus preventing us from proving our facility works! Oh, this is horrible! That poor baby."

"Don't break out the tissues just yet," I announced, as Jillian, the dogs, Officer Sanderson, and I walked through CCCP's front door.

I made the introductions as I struggled to unzip my coat. The chick had changed positions, so that it was now directly over my stomach. If I wasn't careful, my coat would open and the poor chick would fall to the ground. I didn't make it this far just to trip and end up face-planting just before crossing the finish line, thank you very much.

"What are you doing?" Dr. Rozhkov asked. "Why are you taking so long to unzip your ... heavens above!"

There was a collective gasp as I was finally able to work my left arm up under my jacket to support my little hitchhiker. Then, and only then, did I open my coat. There, still sleeping, was the chick.

Everyone present, including Katia, Siggie, Penny, and Isabeau, along with Marianne and Dr. Tanko, surged forward to see for themselves the penguin baby was unharmed. However, the chick's newfound nannies fired off several warning woofs.

"They've become quite attached to him," Jillian explained. "They wouldn't leave Zachary's side."

"I can't believe you found our baby!" Dr. Rozhkov cried. "And he's healthy?"

I looked down at the fluffball of a bird I was holding and shrugged.

"Sure looks like it."

"Where did you find him?" Dr. Rozhkov asked. A single tear was trickling down her cheek.

I pointed at the dogs.

"I can tell you *they* discovered a hidden room behind a closet in Bruce Smith's house. The chick was awake when we arrived, and quite anxious to leave. Then again, it might have something to do with the gas smell. I think it knew it was in danger."

Katia approached first. She glanced at Dr. Rozhkov, who nodded permission.

"May I? We must care for baby. Doctor Tanko? You come with?"

Dr. Tanko handed the bottle of water he had been drinking to Dr. Rozhkov.

"Absolutely. Gently now, don't upset him."

Katia gently reached in and took the sleeping chick out of my jacket. All four keepers immediately headed for the infirmary, with Dr. Tanko hot on their heels.

Marianne sank down into the closest chair. Both eyes were brimming with tears.

"I don't know how you did it," she began, "but you have my eternal thanks."

I pointed at Sherlock and Watson, who were staring at the empty space where they last saw the chick. "You do realize you should be addressing two corgis, don't you? I had absolutely nothing to do with any of their accomplishments."

Marianne was giddy with excitement.

"You did it! Er, Sherlock and Watson did it, with time to spare! Oh, we need to celebrate, and I have just the thing. Tonight, you and Jillian will be our guests of honor for a sumptuous crab feast at Salmon Point Crab. You did say you are a fan of crab?"

"I can eat my weight in crab," I boasted.

"It's the best place to get locally caught seafood. You'll love it! I'm just sorry we can't include *all* the guests of honor."

"A crab dinner? O-ho, you're on!" I exclaimed. I actually felt myself start drooling. "Don't worry about the dogs. I'll give them extra kibble tonight. They'll sleep like babies."

Later, at the encouragement of Dr. Rozhkov, I kept going until I literally felt like the waitress would have to roll me out on a dolly. I think I put away nearly three pounds of crab. Oh, it had to be expensive, and no matter how much Jillian and I tried, Marianne assured me that we could keep going until we either ran out of space or else the restaurant ran out of crab. Very well, challenge accepted.

Everyone was at dinner, and I do mean everyone. Anyone who had helped us in any way, shape, or form had been invited, all the way down to the bearded bartender, Matt, from Burt's Old Time Saloon. I thought for certain he'd decline, since he really didn't know anyone else, but then again, how often are you offered a free crab dinner?

All four animal keepers were there, along with their significant others. That is, except for Katia, who was single. Then again, that might explain why she kept stealing sidelong glances at Matt. Also with us was the good Doctor Tanko, and our new friends, the Fleischmans. Arlen, looking as though she would pop at any moment, and Jason took seats next to us. Jason gave me a fist bump as he ordered himself a beer.

Dinner was fantastic. Freshly-caught Alaskan snow crab ... Mm-mmm! It was a feast that shouldn't be missed. The crab legs were already pre-cut, the butter sat on one of those little warmers, so it was always hot and melty, and no matter how many times I cleared my plate, the waitresses kept bringing more.

Let me tell you, it was a dark day for the local crustacean population. Hours later, right before Jillian and I retired for the night, I actually Googled what was the largest portion of crab ever consumed by a human being.

It was sometime during the third refill of crab when the subject of the unlucky chick was finally brought up.

"I was telling Zachary," Jillian began, "that I don't think I have ever seen something as cute as that baby penguin."

"I wished I could have seen it," Arlen said, sighing.

Katia, Penny, Isabeau, Siggie, and my wife all whipped out their phones and presented them to our pregnant friend. The keepers shared a look and burst into laughter.

"Come see," Katia was saying. "Pictures. We all have some."

Jillian was closest. She slid her phone over, and while Arlen oohed and aahed over the infant penguin, Marianne clinked her glass. She lifted it up, which prompted everyone to mimic her.

"To our new friends from Oregon, and our new

friends we made here, in Sitka. Zack, Jillian, thank you from the bottom of my heart. You came to our aid when we needed it the most, and were able to do what was needed. I wanted to thank the dogs, too, so I placed a few calls and a little bird identified their favorite treats."

"Oh, no," I groaned.

"Oh, yes," Marianne argued. "I ordered several dozen from ... let me see. I wrote it down. Fur, Fins, and Feathers. Sound familiar?"

I sighed. "Yes. Do you have any idea how badly those smell? And do you know what they are?"

Dr. Rozhkov blushed. "Pizzle sticks? Yes, I am aware. You, or rather *they,* have a number of those treats on the way."

Arlen raised a hand. "Excuse me? I'm sorry. Pizzle sticks? What are they, some type of Oregon dog treat?"

I pushed Arlen's hand down. "Trust me, if you don't know, it's best you don't try too hard to figure it out."

Jason's curiosity got the better of him, so he looked up the treat online. When he saw the answer, he burst out laughing. He handed the phone to his wife, who nearly spewed her water when she saw that a pizzle stick was nothing more than a dried *bull penis.*

"What was the deal with that dragon toy?" Jason asked, once the laughter had died down.

"Corgi clues," I answered. "In this case, Sherlock and Watson were telling us to pay attention to dragons. Why? Well, Chris, er, he was CCCP's computer tech, was a fan of them. He was the one who manipulated the computer into turning off the security cameras, so his sister, Shannon, could steal the chick. The corgis wanted us to give the computer a closer look, especially since it had a big dragon on the desktop. And if that wasn't clear enough, Chris has a tattoo of a dragon on his left forearm."

"Incredible," Siggie breathed. The normally reserved keeper took a sip from her glass of wine and shook her head. "I never would have imagined mere dogs could be that smart."

"If you ever want proof of just how intelligent a dog can be," I said, drawing everyone's attention, "hide their favorite treat somewhere in your house, where you know they can find it. Once they do, sit back and enjoy the fun, 'cause each and every consecutive day, that dog will return to that spot to see if there's anything else there."

"No way," Penny said, giggling.

"It's true," Jillian told her. "I pushed a couple of pig ears into the sofa cushions back at our house. Sherlock and Watson check that spot every time they jump onto the couch. I've even caught Sherlock digging into the cushions a few times, so perhaps that isn't the best suggestion?"

"Is *that* why he does that?" I asked, laughing. "I couldn't figure out what kept drawing them back there. I assumed they were looking for a toy or a treat, but every time I checked, I came up empty-handed."

"That's why," Jillian confirmed.

More laughter ensued.

"What about the banana?" Jason asked. "They wouldn't let it go on my boat."

"A banana?" Dr. Tanko asked, certain he had heard wrong. "You are referencing the yellow fruit? I'm sorry, English is not my first language. I wish to understand."

"That's the one," Jason confirmed. "I had one on board *DeeDee*. I hadn't had lunch yet, so I snacked on it while we were cruising around."

"Bruce Smith was, er, *is* a pilot of one of those floater planes," I explained. "His plane is bright yellow, and is nicknamed *Banana Boat*. We kept seeing it overhead, 'cause we're pretty sure Bruce was spying on us."

"And what about all the moose sightings?" Marianne asked.

"The mooses," I chuckled. "They …"

"… *moose*," my wife interrupted.

"Right. That's what I said."

"You said mooses. The plural is *moose*."

I shrugged. "Thought it didn't sound right."

"Didn't you say you're a writer?" Jason asked.

"Yeah, yeah," I mock-grumbled.

Jason snorted with laughter.

Arlen perked up. "What do you write? I've been reading a lot lately. Maybe I've read something from you?"

"Romance novels, if you can believe that," I said.

229

"But not under my name. I use a pseudonym."

Dr. Tanko gave me an encouraging smile. "A romance novelist? I'm sure my wife would know of it. It's her favorite genre."

"Where is she, Malek?" Marianne asked. "Wasn't she able to come?"

"It'd be a rather long way for her to go," Dr. Tanko admitted. "She's visiting her mother, back home in Bauchi."

Jillian nodded. "Nigeria."

Dr. Tanko beamed, flashing a wide smile with sparkling white teeth. "Exactly. You have visited there?"

"I'm afraid not, actually," Jillian said.

"You should. My country is beautiful. You'd love it."

"I'll add it to my places I'd like to visit," Jillian promised.

"What pen name do you use?" one of the keepers asked. I didn't see who asked, but it sounded like Penny.

"Chastity Wadsworth," I said, briefly wondering if anyone at the table might have read a book or two.

Arlen's eyes widened. Katia choked on her cocktail. Penny blushed, and began giggling. Like Arlen, Isabeau's eyes widened with shock. And Siggie, the quiet, introverted penguin keeper choked on her drink, which was rum, by the way. I'm told rinsing one's nasal passages with alcohol can be quite painful by the way, so by all means, *don't try that at home.*

"You?" Katia stammered. "You wrote *Misty Moors*?"

"I did," I confirmed, nodding.

Dr. Tanko smiled politely. "Ah, I'm afraid I do not know that name."

A thought occurred.

"How about Jim McGee?"

The Nigerian doctor hesitated, and his eyes registered shock.

"I have, yes. But, you couldn't be the one who wrote …?"

"*Heart of Éire.* Yes, that's me, too. I'm currently working on the sequel, *Spirit of Éire.*"

"I knew we had a celebrity in our midst," Marianne began, "but I thought it was the dogs. You're a fantastic writer, Mr. Anderson."

"Thank you. It means a lot."

"You never answered me about the mooses," Jason reminded me. He noticed both my wife—and his—watching him intently. "I mean, moose. What about the moose clues?"

"Bruce Smith wore a moose hat," I said.

"A moose hat," Jason repeated, frowning. "I don't get it. One of those ghastly tourist souvenirs, with the felt antlers?"

"Huh? No, sorry. I meant, he had on a baseball cap with a moose on the front."

"It does seem strange that Sherlock and Watson would focus on moose as often as they did when the clue would be fairly trivial," Jillian said, frowning.

"Think we're missing something?" I asked.

My wife nodded. "I do, but I don't know what. I'm sorry."

"I can answer that," a new voice announced.

We all looked up and saw another friendly face approach.

I rose to my feet and grasped his hand.

"Officer Sanderson! Glad you could join us!"

"Thank you for the invite," Ron said, nodding. "This is my girlfriend, Jessica. I'm sorry we're late."

A short brunette girl, who looked to be no older than a high school student, smiled and waved at everyone.

"Please, call me Jessie. It's nice to meet y'all."

Once the latest additions had seated themselves, we all turned to Ron.

"You were saying? About the moose reference?"

"Oh, it's nothing that major," Ron assured us. He slid Jessie's chair out and helped her get situated. Once she was, he helped himself to a fresh cheddar biscuit from a nearby basket. "Turns out Bruce Smith sometimes goes by Moose. The captain told me. Anyway, he's got quite a temper. He's been arrested nearly half a dozen times alone in the last two years."

"A nickname," I said, shrugging. "Moose? How did he get that name? From his temper?"

"Umm, let's just attribute his name to his uncanny ability to mimic a moose's mating call," Ron chortled.

"A moose mating call," I carefully repeated. As much as I tried, I couldn't piece together what that was supposed to mean.

"His ability to clear out a room," Ron added.

Jessie's eyes widened. "Ronald, not at the dinner table!"

Ron's blush deepened. He mumbled an apology and focused his attention on the basket of biscuits.

The light dawned, and suddenly, I knew what he was talking about. A moose call? Looks like our pal Bruce had something in common with Watson!

"I get it!" I exclaimed, laughing out loud. "He's gassy, with an audible factor well above normal. That's hysterical!"

The table fell silent as all eyes turned to me.

"Zachary!" Jillian hissed.

"Oh. Uh, sorry. Should've kept that one to myself, huh?"

Ron and Jason were both staring at their drinks. Each refused eye contact.

"Don't even think about laughing at that," Arlen warned.

Jason tried to shrug nonchalantly. Jessie said something similar to Ron.

"I promise that's all I'll say about it, but I do have one final question. How did the local police figure that out?"

"He's had a few minor run-ins," Ron answered, discreetly wiping the corners of his eyes with his napkin. "Usually drunken brawls. Each time he was in, we ended up having to open all windows and break out the Febreze. I don't know what his diet is, but he sure needs to change it. That's the moose reference your dogs wanted us to find?"

"As I've said quite a few times since I was talked into adopting two corgis, I'm not sure how we would've known that. Thanks for the explanation. Hey, I don't suppose you guys have any leads on him? Any chance of apprehending him? I don't like the fact that he literally threw his two kids under the bus and made his getaway."

"And, he blew up his house in an attempt to kill the chick and cover his tracks," Jillian reminded us.

"*Da*," Katia said. "I owe him …"

"You owe him?" Penny interrupted, appalled. "Why would you say that?"

Katia held up a finger. "Not finished. I owe him sandwich."

The table fell silent.

"You owe him a sandwich?" I repeated. The clouds cleared and I realized what the poor woman was trying to say. "You left out a word. Would you mean a *knuckle sandwich*?"

"*Da*. A beating. I owe him beating for scaring baby."

Penny's frown vanished. "Oh, I'm so sorry. Yes, you're right. And do you know what? I'll help you do it."

Katia nodded and held her fist out. "*Da*, sister."

Jillian suddenly held up a hand.

"Wait a moment. All the clues have been accounted for, and explained, save one."

"What'd we miss?" I asked.

"The drug store," Jillian said. "Sherlock and Watson stopped at that little shop and wouldn't move until you took a picture."

Intrigued, I went through the photo album on my phone until I found it.

"The apothecary. You're right. I had forgotten about that one."

"How does a drug store tie in to the theft of one of our penguins?" Dr. Rozhkov asked.

"I don't know," I admitted. "It really doesn't matter, does it? We have the chick back, and we did it before your inspector shows up tomorrow. I say we don't worry about it."

My wife frowned. "Zachary, every case I have ever seen you work with the dogs has an explanation for *every* clue. This drug store means something. So, what we have to ask ourselves is, what's left? What hasn't been addressed?"

The table went quiet for a second time. I was about to shrug when I realized there was, indeed, one loose end we had yet to tie up.

"Smith," I said. "Moose-man is still at large."

Jason snorted. "Moose-man?"

"Hey, there's nothing wrong with making this fun for me, is there?" I grinned.

Jason held out a hand and waited for me to hand him my phone. He and Arlen studied it for a few moments before he handed it back.

"You're telling me that *that* picture, that drug store, will somehow help you capture the mastermind behind this whole operation? It'll tell you where you can find this Bruce Smith character?"

I looked uncertainly at Jillian. My wife was silent as she considered her answer.

"With Sherlock and Watson, there are always answers to everything they do. If they want us to look at something, then rest assured, that particular clue *will* play some part in solving the case."

"This case is already solved," I pointed out.

"But not with a loose end," Jillian argued. "Unless we can deduce how a pharmacy could possibly tie in to the theft of the penguin, then I can only assume it has something to do with the person who pulled it off. In this case, this may very well be the clue we need in order to locate our culprit."

"I'm all ears," Ron said. "If you can figure out how we can find Mr. Bruce Smith, and get him back to Sitka, then the police department would be in your debt. As it stands right now, the perp got away. Our captain is not a fan of letting criminals escape, especially under his watch."

"Get him back?" I repeated. Rusty wheels began to turn. "The no-fly ban is still in effect, isn't it?"

Officer Sanderson nodded. "It is."

"And what happens if a pilot chooses to disregard that order and takes their plane up anyway?" I asked.

Ron's mouth closed with a snap.

"That's a damn good question. I don't know."

Jillian pulled out her phone. "I'm on it. Give me a moment. Hmm, interesting. It says here whenever a no-fly ban goes into effect, that means the affected area becomes a no-fly zone. Should a pilot enter a no-fly zone, then fighter jets typically appear and escort the plane out. Should the plane refuse, then the jets will fire flares and force you to land at the nearest military base."

"Is there one here?" I asked.

"Air Station Sitka," Jillian reported. "Based on everything I've read, if you're a pilot, you do *not* mess with a no-fly zone."

"That confirms it," I said, growing excited.

"What confirms *what*?" Jason asked.

"The clue. Bruce Smith—he's still in the area. Honey, you're right. That last clue must help us locate our missing man. Think about it. Smith is an experienced pilot. He knows if he tries to fly anywhere in his plane, it'll be tracked on radar, and the authorities will go after him. No, he needs to lay low, and let things cool down. We know he was in the area, since we watched him fly away from his house, yesterday. He wouldn't have made it far. No, he's around here somewhere."

Ron straightened in his chair.

"Assuming you're right, do you have any idea how many places there are to hide? Alaska is the largest state in the union. Islands are everywhere, *and* he's flying a floater. Can we say needle in a haystack?"

"That's where the dogs come in," I said. "The last clue? We have to figure out what it means. I think Jillian is right: the clue will lead us to Smith."

Plates were stacked and pushed out of the way. Mistakenly thinking our group was preparing to leave, our waitress hurried over to start clearing plates.

"There's no rush to leave, guys," the girl began.

"Oh, we're not going anywhere," I assured her. "We just need a little room."

"Oh, uh, okay. Would anyone like me to top off their drinks?"

Drinks were filled, additional bottles of beer arrived, and a new bottle of wine was uncorked for Dr. Tanko and Isabeau. As for me, I sipped my (full) soda and took a breath, eager to begin.

"Okay, this question is for anyone who can answer it." I moved my glass to the center of the table. "This is Sitka. Katia is currently sitting north, and I'm south. What island is closest to us and where's its approximate location?"

Jason was shaking his head, and Ron was frowning.

"There are not enough glasses in this restaurant to properly represent all the islands in this area," the policeman told us.

I pulled my glass back. "Hmm, okay. Are all of them inhabited?"

At least three-quarters of the table started shaking their heads.

"Can you land one of those pontoon planes at

any of the islands?" Jillian asked. "I mean, I know there's water, so Smith should be able to. I guess I'm asking if there are any with the ability to moor a boat, or in this case, a plane."

"Yes," Jason confirmed. "I've seen quite a few. Many people have homes on those islands, houses that are off the grid. People like their isolation, and Alaska is a fantastic place to live if you don't mind getting your hands dirty."

Sighing, I came to a decision.

"We're back to the clue. All right, everyone. It's time to put your thinking caps on. Drug stores. How could they possibly help us locate our pal Smith?"

Ron held out a hand. "You've been taking pictures as you go? Smart move. Did you take one of this drug store?"

"I did. Here, take a look."

"Hmm. Okay, you're Sherlock and Watson's owner. You've been on cases before, right?"

"Quite a few," I nodded.

"Can I assume you don't always identify the purpose of the picture until sometime later?"

"Spot on, Jason. Wait. Where are you going with this?"

Jason tapped my phone.

"How do you know your dogs want you to focus on this store?"

Arlen looked at her husband.

"What else could be determined by looking at that photo? After all, it *is* just a store."

"Well, at no point do I see the word *drug store*. I do see apothecary, though. So, for instance, is there an island called Apothecary Island?"

Jillian was nodding.

"I see where you're going with this. You make a fine point. And, for the record, is there?"

Arlen pulled her own phone out.

"I can check. Let's see. Wow. I never knew there were so many islands. It says here that there are over eighteen-hundred named islands, with many more unnamed. And … it's official. I don't see an island with that name. It was a good idea, love."

Jason shrugged and reached for his beer.

"Well, I know this a long shot," I began, "but could there be a Drugstore Island?"

This earned me a round of laughter. And, consequently, there wasn't.

"Synonyms," I said. "What are some synonyms for drug store? Arlen? You already have your phone out. Will you research the names as they're suggested?"

"Of course."

"Awesome. Thanks. Now, I doubt there's a Narcotics Island. Or, is there?"

Arlen shook her head.

"No, sorry."

"Pharmacy?" Penny suggested.

No such island.

"Drugs," Jillian mused. "Is there a Hippy Island?"

"Ooooo, good answer," Arlen said, without looking up. Jason snorted with laughter. "What?

What'd I say?"

"You've been watching *Family Feud*, haven't you?"

Arlen grinned sheepishly. "When you're this far along, everything hurts, so I try not to move too much. What do I end up doing? Watching TV and reading books. The answer is no, by the way. No Hippy Island listed."

"Customer," Katia said. When no one said anything, the Russian keeper continued. "Maybe customer? Him buy drugs, have records with computer?"

"Prescriptions!" Jillian exclaimed. "Good job, Katia! Only problem is, I think trying to get that kind of information would require a warrant, wouldn't it? And as long as we're at it, perhaps we should check doctor offices? They write prescriptions, which are then filled at pharmacies. Perhaps they might be able to tell us something we didn't know?"

Ron reached for his phone. "I'm on it. We'll let the captain make that call."

The officer rose to his feet and walked outside to place the call.

"I like where this is going," I said, giving Katia a smile. "Let's keep it up. What else can we try?"

Jillian held out a hand. I passed her my phone and watched her peruse the pictures. She returned to the photo of the apothecary shop and fell silent.

"The captain is friends with the owner," Ron announced, as he returned to our table. Sliding out his chair, he sat down and took Jessie's hand in his own. "He called and was able to confirm that Bruce Smith did *not* have any prescriptions there, and from what he was told, no one by that name ever had a record in their computer system. I'm told there's a security system in place, with cameras covering every angle. The owner is willing to review the footage, but it kinda sounds like it might be a moot point. As for other clinics, there are over twenty-five registered physicians in Sitka. And, it's past five, so all will be closed."

"There must be *something*," I insisted.

Jillian suddenly grasped my arm.

"The name. The name of the shop!"

"Apothecary," I recalled. "We already checked."

My wife shook her lovely head.

"Lotus Blossom. The name of the store? Lotus Blossom Apothecary. Arlen, could you see if there's a Lotus Blossom Island? Or maybe just Blossom?"

"No on both counts," Arlen reported, several minutes later.

There was a collective groan of dismay.

"But …"

Heads turned. Eyes focused on Jason's wife.

"… there *is* a Lotus Island."

A stunned silence fell over the table.

"Where?" I cautiously asked.

Arlen slid her fingers along her cell's display.

"Guys, it doesn't look far! Lotus Island is in Islet Passage. According to this, Lotus Island is a tiny chunk of land a hop, skip, and jump from

Sosnovoi. Er, that'd be to the north of Sosnovoi."

"Sosnovoi?" Ron repeated. "That's only ten miles from here, as the crow flies!" The police officer hurriedly rose, grabbed his phone, and kissed his girlfriend. "Be right back. I *know* the captain will want to know about this."

"I sure hope we find him," Dr. Rozhkov said. "That man doesn't deserve to walk free."

I raised my beer. "Here, here. Hey, Katia, could I ask you something?"

"*Da*. What you wish to know?"

"The chick? How's it doing? Is it all right? I guess I'm asking if the poor thing was treated well."

"*Da*. Healthy. How you say …? Little bit not right weight."

"Underweight," Jillian guessed.

Katia nodded. "*Da*. Is no worry. Dr. Tanko say chick fine."

I let out the breath I had been holding. "Oh, that's good to hear."

"I hope they find him," Jillian said. "I don't like knowing that man is out there, free to do whatever he likes."

Ron returned about ten minutes later, sporting a huge grin on his face.

"You've got some good news, don't you?" I asked, eager for some good news.

"They're already moving on this!"

"Did your captain mention how long it'll take before they know something?" I asked.

Ron shrugged. "He had a team standing by,

including a contingent of boats. He was already reaching out to them before our own call was even finished. It's been, what, about twenty minutes? If you account for the time it takes for the captain to make it down to the docks, and then the boat ride out to Lotus, then I'd say we should hear something right about ..."

I don't know how he did it. Officer Sanderson had absolutely perfect timing. Ron's phone began ringing. The policeman smiled at all of us, glanced at the display, and started to wander off. However, he only made it a few steps before he stopped, said something into the phone, and finished the call. Once he was back at the table, he held up a fist, which I immediately bumped.

"That was the captain. They came, they found, and they took him down. Bruce Smith is in custody, and from what I hear, he is absolutely furious. He kept demanding we tell him how we knew where to find him."

I pumped a fist in the air. "That's totally awesome news! Good job, guys!" I noticed my soda glass was full and briefly wondered when it had been filled. "Here's to a job well done!"

Glasses were lifted, bottles were clinked together, and wine glasses came dangerously close to sloshing over.

"One more thing, guys," Ron added. "I've been authorized to tell you tonight's dinner is on the Sitka Police Department."

I held up a hand. "Waitress? Hand me a dessert

menu, would you?"

EPILOGUE

T hey are magnificent creatures, aren't they?"
Jillian was saying.

"I had heard somewhere that the adults could reach a height of four feet tall, and weigh around fifty pounds."

"You didn't believe it?" my wife asked.

"Seeing is believing," I said.

We were standing outside one of the exhibits at CCCP. This one, according to the sign posted at the view point, was the Buzz pen. At least, that's what it said once we brushed the snow off of it.

Winter was pretty much in full swing, having come a few days early. Thankfully, we weren't in any danger of getting snowed in. Yet. However, I didn't want to press our luck, so we would be departing for the airport in about fifteen minutes. We were back here, at CCCP, due to Dr. Rozhkov's request. And, since we were outside, we were both bundled up like our lives depended on it: long-sleeve sweaters, winter coats, thermal undies, wind breakers … heck, I think Jillian was wearing them all. At the same time. As for me, I had on my regular black sweatshirt, jeans, boots, and a thin pair of gloves. Jillian thought I was nuts, but for me, it was plenty warm.

Sherlock and Watson were also wearing their winter attire. Both had on their snow booties, which was hysterical to watch them walk with them on, and their full length coats. A light dusting of snow had turned each of them white, which had the corgis periodically shaking the small white flakes off every couple of minutes.

"There you are," Marianne announced, as she and two of the keepers, Katia and Isabeau, arrived. "Again, thank you so much for saving our butts. Well, mine most of all."

"How'd it go with the inspector?" Jillian asked.

"He left about an hour ago. We won't get the official results for a few more days, but he told me he saw nothing to prevent him from recommending our accreditation. So, for that, thank you."

"How's the chick?" I asked.

Marianne motioned the keepers over. Isabeau unzipped her jacket to reveal the sleeping chick.

"He's doing quite well. He's put back on the weight he's lost and then some."

I pointed at the sleeping baby.

"Is that how you're supposed to carry them? You mean I guessed right?"

Katia and Isabeau both laughed.

"*Mon Dieu, non*. We saw how he responded to

you, *non*? If you can do it, then so can we."

"Bruce Smith pled guilty," Marianne told us.

I nodded. "Good. Glad to hear he was man enough to 'fess up to his crimes."

"Why did he do it?" Jillian asked. "What grudge could he have had against that poor baby?"

Isabeau zipped her jacket back up.

"He claims it was all my fault," Marianne said, with a sigh. "He claims that the land I bought, the ones that came with water rights, never should have been sold to me. Please bear in mind, I never had any intention of using them. I just wanted the ability to, if the situation ever called for it."

"What did Bruce have against you and your private water access?" I wanted to know.

"He thought we were some huge corporation," Dr. Rozhkov explained. "I think he thought we were some nameless entity that was snapping up local land with the intent to … I don't know, put hotels up? Bring in local franchise restaurants? Who knows. All I know is his business is based in tourism, and he thought we were ruining the town."

"Which you're not," I pointed out.

"You know that. I know that. He didn't."

We watched the penguins in silence for several more minutes. I heard the dogs' collars jingle, and I knew it was time to get them out of the cold. I turned to our new friend and held out a hand.

"Marianne, it's been a pleasure. I'm so glad we could help you guys out. Isabeau? Katia? I hope you don't mind, but I'm planning on creating a couple of characters in my next *Misty Moors* sequel based off of you guys."

Both keepers gasped with surprise.

"*Da!* Is much thankful!"

Isabeau elbowed her in the stomach.

"*Mais oui*, that is the wrong word, *mon amie*."

"Appreciate! Is much appreciate!"

I smiled. "Close enough. Thanks, guys! Keep in touch, okay?"

They then gave Sherlock and Watson some last minute scratches before we headed out. Once we were at the airport, and literally waiting to board our plane, I heard the telltale sounds of a cricket chirping, which could only mean someone had just texted me. Sighing, I pulled out my cell and glanced at the display. It was from my friend, Vance, the PV detective. What I saw made my blood boil.

YOU BACK? ROBBERY. CBN.

"You've *got* to be kidding me."

Having heard my outburst, Jillian came up behind me to lean over my shoulder so she could see for herself what was on my phone. Once she read the message, instead of freaking out, like I thought she would, her eyes practically flashed with fire.

"Cookbook Nook has been robbed? Seriously?"

AUTHOR'S NOTE

Just a few quick notes. I'll have you know, there actually *is* such a place as Lotus Island, Alaska, but unfortunately, it is nowhere near the town of Sitka. So, for the purposes of the story, it was plucked off the map and transported nearly two-thousand miles away, to a location just a smidge north of Sosnovoi Island, a part of Tongass National Forest. For all you Alaskan natives, don't hate me.

Ainsworth Lodge Island was based off of Fin Lodge Island. If you ever take an Alaskan cruise, and are fortunate enough to stop in Sitka, that particular excursion can't be beat. You've got a guided boat tour, wildlife watching, whale spotting, and a finale which consists of a stop at a private island for a crab feast. Trust me, it's just as good as it sounds. The food is awesome, the scenery is breath-taking, and the experience is worth every penny.

What's next for Zack and the gang? Well, as you just saw, while they were away, in Alaska, someone decided to break into Cookbook Nook and trash the place. Why would anyone want to do that? What's the motive? Well, Sherlock and Watson are more than happy to come to Jillian's aid, as is most of the town, if you must know. Watch for *Case of the Ice Cream Crime.*

After this, I'll be tackling CCF19, *Case of the Hobbit Heist.* As the name suggests, an element of fantasy is involved, but that might be because for the first time in three years, a full-fledged comic con is returning to southern Oregon. As usual when it comes to Zack, things don't go as planned.

If you liked the book, please consider leaving a review wherever you purchased it. Reviews are what helps authors stand out. There are many books to choose from, so allow me to thank you for picking up a copy of mine. Until next time!

Happy reading!

J.
December, 2022

Zack and the dogs will be back in their next adventure,
Case of the Ice Cream Crime **(Corgi Case files #18)!**

Meanwhile, catch up on the Corgi Case Files Series
Available in e-book and paperback

Case of the One-Eyed Tiger
Case of the Fleet-Footed Mummy
Case of the Holiday Hijinks
Case of the Pilfered Pooches
Case of the Muffin Murders
Case of the Chatty Roadrunner
Case of the Highland House Haunting
Case of the Ostentatious Otters
Case of the Dysfunctional Daredevils
Case of the Abandoned Bones
Case of the Great Cranberry Caper
Case of the Shady Shamrock
Case of the Ragin' Cajun
Case of the Missing Marine
Case of the Stuttering Parrot
Case of the Rusty Sword

If you enjoy Epic Fantasy, check out Jeff's other series:

Bakkian Chronicles
The Prophecy
Insurrection
Amulet of Aria

Tales of Lentari Series
Coming Summer 2023

Dragons of Andela Series
Coming Fall/Winter 2023

Made in the USA
Middletown, DE
01 September 2024

60171834R00158